LOVERS AND MONSTERS

A Deathless Love Short Story Collection

ZORA FOX

CONTENTS

WELCOME TO THE EIGHT REALMS

A land of gods and goddesses—a savage, beautiful collection of islands in the Corae Sea. The stories here are violent, with explicit sexual content not intended for anyone under 18. These books about deathless love feature dark, often twisted romances. Enter at your own risk.

ZENIA

Ruled by Thenios, God-King of lightning

APHRISO

Ruled by Cytherea, goddess of pleasure

ERISET

Contested land, ruled by Ares and Bellona, god and goddess of war

MENOS

Ruled by Scira, goddess of wisdom

NALIA

Ruled by Basileus, god of the ocean

HYPERION

Ruled by Lox, god of the sun

KANTHAROS

Ruled by Vesta, goddess of hearth and home

FAR REALM

Ruled by Hades, god of the dead

Content warnings for these story of deathless love: listed before each story individually, but all include explicit sex (often with multiple people, monsters, or BDSM elements) and strong language

READER BEWARE!

Here's the part where I remind you that these stories are erotica. They have lots and lots of the spicy stuff we love. If you don't want to read about A) characters from the longer Deathless Love stories that might spoil the plot, or B) smut in general, turn around. This is your final warning.

In these pages, you'll encounter a variety of stories that range from the romantic to the twisted. Things these short stories have in common:

- Fantasy world—all the characters exist in the same mythology-inspired world ruled by gods and demi-gods called the deathless
- Consent, including age of consent—I'm not about non-con or dub-con
- Lots of smut

That's it.
Close the door and enjoy, Foxy!

HADES'S SHADOW

Hades's shadow wants to try something new with Persephone while Hades watches.

Inspired by Hades and Persephone's story in *Flowers and the Far Realm*, this story includes explicit sex, strong language, voyeurism, pain kink, a *big* monster, masturbation, and aftercare

Hades sat on the sofa, spreading out like a predator at ease in his immaculate suit. I'd spent all day underground, working on the space I'd created for human spirits, and Hades had spent the day putting out fires between rival demi-gods vying for territory. We were both tired and aching to unwind. It was good to see his face.

He gave a barely there smile, reached for the glass on the end table, and took a sip. This relaxed version of Hades was my favorite. Well, no, there was another, even better version that I might get to see tonight now that we were back together in our massive suite.

"The shadow wants to try things. I want to let him." He tilted his head at me. "Should I?"

He looked so good that I sat on his lap and gave him a kiss.

"Is that a yes?" he whispered, breath sharp and spicy.

"Only the shadow?" I teased. I couldn't count the number of times Hades and his shadow had taken me at once. It was violent and heavenly at once. I craved them like I'd craved nothing else.

Hades and I had had sex alone, without his dark shadow self, but I'd never been railed only by the shadow. What would that be like? My stomach tightened with nerves and anticipation. I smoothed the skirt of my dark pink dress. Hades's eyes followed the movement of my hands. A low rumble growled deep in his throat.

Biting my lip, I met his gray eyes. They pinned me in place, hungry.

"Only the shadow. For now," he answered.

I adjusted my hips on his lap. "You'll watch."

His answering look confirmed my suspicion. He moved my hair off my shoulder and slid his fingers down my arm, possessive. "I'll supervise. Can't have him hurt you."

Unless she wants it. That was what the shadow said the first time both of them took me. Gods, that was...

"Yes," I said.

"Yes, he can try something?"

"Yes."

"Tell me if you want him to stop."

I nodded, getting more excited. Hades himself was already brutal, but sophisticated and compassionate toward his subjects. The shadow was made of the darkest parts of him, the parts that craved blood and sex and power. It was unpredictable, demanding. A creature version of the man before me.

Hades's shadow could hurt me—*had* hurt me—but never intentionally. If Hades was possessive, his shadow was feral. But, no matter what the shadow did, I couldn't die. We were all deathless gods.

Hades lifted me gently off his lap. He stood beside me. His eyes had gone dark, everything about him a cultured, barely restrained mass of desperation. It was the look he got before he grabbed me and made me his.

I inhaled a quiet gasp as he loomed over me. The scent of mint filled my nose.

"Now," he whispered, toying with the straps of my dress, "he's going to be rough with you."

"Good."

He thumbed my bottom lip. "Bad girl." Then he smiled, sloppy. Reaching behind me for the buttons of my dress, he pressed our bodies together—my small, full frame against his hard, muscular one. His fingers undid each clasp, his breath growing shallower and more annoyed by the second. This side of Hades loved order, sought it compulsively, like the way he folded his clothes whenever he undressed.

But he craved chaos too.

With a grunt, he finished the final button. That noise meant his shadow self had ripped out of him. Yes, there he was. Like a black outline of naked Hades with elongated claws for fingers and pointed teeth.

Hades gripped my chin, forcing me to look at him while the shadow circled. "We have... monstrous appetites."

"I have lots of proof," I teased, the words emerging breathless. Why was he saying this now? I'd been in the Far Realm a year. The underground area for the human spirits to inhabit was almost finished. It was the best work I'd ever done, far outweighing my work on the queen's garden in

Kantharos. Hades and I would marry once it was done. His shadow had joined us for many monstrous sessions in that bedroom.

The look in his eyes said he meant something different this time. My stomach squirmed. "You warned me in the beginning, remember?"

Hades leaned to speak low in my ear. "There's more we want to do with you." The words were careful, with a telltale rasp that meant the idea turned him on enough to barely remain in control.

I kissed him lightly on the lips. "There's more I want to do with you too." He felt so warm and solid against me. It took willpower not to sink to my knees before him and find out just how hard I made him.

"Persephone," he chided.

"Hades," I shot back, imitating his tone.

"Enough," came the growling voice of the shadow.

Hades looked at the shadow over my shoulder. He nodded.

A hiss of excitement emitted from the shadow's throat. I barely had time to turn before he had me in his arms. From the corner of my eye, I saw Hades sit on the sofa again to watch.

Hades's suite was large, dark, and beautiful, like him. There was the sitting room, where we were now, high enough for a visible second floor, accessible by tight spiral staircases. Under the large second floor balcony (complete with a pool overlooking the Far Realm—I dreamed about that sometimes) was his bedroom. An enormous, round bed with silken black sheets was the main feature in there.

The black, skull-and-rose headboard had patches of thick, mossy greenery. So did the floor upstairs. Both were my doing. When I first discovered I could coax life out of almost nothing, I could barely control tht power when Hades plunged inside me.

I thought the shadow would whisk me to the bed, but he didn't. Instead, he stayed in the sitting room area, like we were a show for Hades to watch. That didn't sound as comfortable, but Hades hadn't promised comfort. Besides, I liked when they took me rough. It was all the fantasies I hadn't fully admitted to myself when I read naughty books in the pristine garden before Hades stole me away.

The shadow grimaced down at me. The rock-hard outline of his cock pressed against my belly. Nails scraped my back as the shadow tore the rest of my dress away. I could picture Hades wanting to say something, but resisting. The dress could be fixed, although that ripping sound was pretty loud.

"Mine. You're mine," the shadow rasped feverishly. "All to myself." His hands with those long nails felt their way down my back to my ass.

Anticipation and hot desire made me wet and responsive. When he separated my cheeks and gave me a hard slap on one side, I gasped and wriggled in his hold.

I felt every muscle hard against me and realized the shadow usually took the back if they were with me together. I always faced Hades. Now I faced the shadow.

"Does your body want mine?" he muttered, breathless.

The shadow was all feral need. His words were eager, almost unconscious. He was *doing*, not speaking. So instead of answering in words, I reached for him.

"She wants it," he breathed, toothy smile growing too big. This was the face that frightened children and gods.

"Fuck me," I whispered, feeling wicked.

An eloquent exhale from Hades on the sofa told me he approved.

The shadow picked me up like I weighed as much as a flower and set me on his hips. Hades had done this too. I could do this. Bounce on his cock.

I groaned as he jammed himself into me. The shadow was never gentle. He entered in one thrust.

A pinch of sharp claws against my bare back told me his fingers had grown longer. Long enough to wrap around my waist and enclose my body. My eyes widened. Hades had never done that.

"Let me see her face," Hades commanded.

"Demanding," muttered the shadow, rotating so Hades could see us in profile.

Hades looked as if checking for something, then nodded again.

What...?

The shadow began to grow. For a disorienting second, I panicked. I was rising toward the second floor, caught in the hands of a monster. He was twice as tall as Hades. And—oh!—he wasn't only growing taller. His cock was... oh gods! He expanded inside me, stretching my walls, pushing deeper, swelling until I could barely breathe. Whimpering, I struggled to make room for him. My head fell back. It hurt.

"Want to be... fucked?" asked the shadow, gripping me harder and sliding me up his long dick.

I shut my eyes tight and nodded.

When he slammed me down, I screamed. He was so hard, it felt like going down a slide or—I didn't know—getting impaled. It was torture. I wanted more.

"Wet wet wet for me," he chanted, picking me up again and pushing me all the way down on his cock again.

I writhed, my legs kicking out. I wasn't grounded, except

for the tight hold around my ribs. His thumbs squeezed just below my breasts.

His movements grew more frantic. Every time he picked me up, I could nearly see up onto the second floor. He was enormous.

I was sobbing, begging incoherent things as he pumped me on his huge shaft.

"Bigger? How much space is in there?" he rumbled.

He grunted with the force of the next thrust.

Tears streamed down my face. "Uh huh... oh!"

"Don't break her. Don't split her open."

I cracked open my eyes to see Hades below me, dick out, palming himself as he watched half-lidded.

The shadow slid me all the way down his slippery cock again. All the way up and all the way down. Harder. Faster. Harder until I was smacking against his groin and screaming whenever he pierced into me. It was like he was telling Hades off, that I wouldn't break.

But I might.

Would I mind?

The thought was ludicrous. Of course I shouldn't want to be split open by a monster shadow's cock, but a dark part of me wanted everything he had to give, even if it meant more pain. It was Hades, and I wanted all of him, even the darkest parts. To me, they were all unbearably sexy.

The head pulsed inside me. It was growing again.

The shadow licked his lips, chest heaving as he paused to stare at me. We rose to the second floor. This was nearly as big as he'd been when I'd summoned him to help close Abaddon, the god prison. Why hadn't I thought about his ability to change whenever we had sex? He could fuck me with the biggest cock among the gods, if he wanted to.

I struggled and strained, gripping the long fingers that held me in place. Widening my legs didn't help much.

He gave a dark chuckle. "She wants more."

With a start, I realized he held me in one massive hand. Sharp claws reached around my front, and I rested in his palm.

"Fingers," Hades warned.

The razor-like nails subsided a little until his fingers were less monstrous. It was a good thing. He held me out, half-impaled, and found my throbbing clit. I arched back violently.

I had to sync my breaths with his thrusts. Or, maybe I didn't. Regardless, when he slammed me down, air forced from my lungs. I was flying and falling, pumping against his cock until I could hardly see. He went faster, matching my desperate, uneven noises as he chased his own release.

Leaning back like this, I could see the expanse of his muscular chest, his abs, his arms as he held me. Still Hades. Just... gods... so big...

With a hard grunt, he used my body to stroke his cock in jerky movements. His free hand flew to hold onto the upper floor as he jammed into me one more time and shot his cum inside.

Slowly, he shrank. His hard dick shrank. Hands held me instead of enormous claws. The shadow licked his lips. "Delicious."

I slid off him, shakily, to the ground.

Hades, hard and half-clothed, caught me. "Brave girl," he breathed warm in my ear. "Are you all right?"

I still couldn't speak. I ached all over. My sex hurt. My skin was sensitive. Was I all right?

When I didn't answer, Hades made me meet his eyes. The shadow was gone. Satisfied and back inside Hades's skin, probably.

"Unbelievable," I croaked.

Hades smirked. "I didn't think you'd like that one."

"He was so huge!" I fell against Hades, nestling my cheek against his chest.

"Can I still have a piece of you?"

"Always," I murmured, sleepy.

He scooped me up and carried me across to the bedroom, where he set me down. Black silk sheets washed around me. He'd need to get them cleaned after this. I was a mess, but I was too wrung out to care.

Hades bent down close to my ear. "Did he only take, or did he give?"

I turned to kiss him on the scruffy cheek. "You couldn't tell?" I teased.

He made a noise in his throat. Straightening, leaving me cold enough for my nipples to harden again, he removed his jacket, his shirt, his pants, which had been pulled partially down already. His cock was rod-straight, not strong enough to hold me up, as the shadow's had been, but my favorite. I opened my mouth, half-delirious.

"No," he said, voice low. "You were good for him, so I'll be good to you."

I smiled.

He smiled back, lowering himself between my sprawled legs. "You're so stretched out."

"Shadow," I murmured.

He closed his lips over my clit, flicking his tongue over the sensitive point.

My fingers closed in a fist over the cool sheets. With my neck straining in pleasure, I looked down at him. He met my eyes and groaned. The vibration ricocheted through my pussy, up my spine, and made me shiver. His tongue went faster.

I was sore, but Hades felt so good. He always felt so good. Whether he held me against his chest in bed as we slept or gripped my neck as he rammed into me from behind, he always felt good.

I hummed, noise pitching higher, as he chased my release. His fingers dug into my thighs as he held me open. My breaths came quicker.

He adjusted the angle of his head just slightly and—there! I bucked and trembled, sweet aching agony racing through my body. He suctioned hard, tongue working over the spot I needed.

My hand found his dark hair, pressing him harder between my legs. Whimpering, I writhed and relived how the shadow had impaled me on his stiff cock, running me up and down his huge length. And I broke. Mouth opened. Eyes rolled back, belly shuddering.

Hades rose, licking his lips.

"That's it," he muttered, rough, wild, and distracted as the shadow's voice. "That's good. Persephone, stay there."

I couldn't do much else. I relaxed into the sheets. Hades stood at the end of the bed, between my open legs. His dick pointed to the upper floor, rigid and heavy as a beam. I knew from experience how soft his skin was on the outside but how unbreakably hard within.

His eyes fell again to my pussy, probably gaping from the treatment I'd gotten from the shadow. It was horrible and wonderful and gods I wanted it to happen again. Just not for a couple more days, judging from how my walls still pulsed painfully from being filled so full.

Hades gripped himself and started pumping his hand up and down. Cum leaked from the head before he even started.

I simply reclined, watching him. His chest and arms flexed

with the seriousness of making himself come. He started making delicious noises, bearded lips parting. At the sound of his groans, my lips curved up. I couldn't help it. Nothing was as sexy as Hades, the god other gods feared, coming apart because of me. His grunts and moans were my favorite sounds.

Wildness took over and he braced himself with one hand on the bed as the shadow had braced himself on the upper floor—they were the same person, after all. His hand flew over his cock, wetness slicking down. Thrusting into his hand as he stroked himself, he finally lost control, shooting white cum all over my stomach.

I drew a finger through the mess and popped it cheekily into my mouth.

"Dirty girl," Hades repeated, swooping down to kiss me.

I squealed with pleasure and returned his kiss open-mouthed.

He sank onto the bed beside me, out of breath. It looked like he wanted to say a thousand things as his eyes roved over me, but he said nothing at all. Contentment warmed his features.

"I love you too," I said, running a hand down his side. He was so beautiful.

He kissed me and got out of bed. "Time to clean you up." Pausing, he turned. "Or would you prefer the pool?"

I grinned. "Pool, please."

He took my hand. In a blink and a gasp, we appeared in the pool on the upper floor. Hades held his arms around me in the warm water. Only Hades and I could travel through the air that way in his palace. It was warded to anybody else. Just another way I was so, so lucky.

Water seeping around us, I leaned my head back on his shoulder.

"Are you still in pain, Persephone?" he asked in that deep, cultured voice I could eat up like strawberries and cream.

"Yes, but that's all right."

He smiled against my ear, fingers lowering to explore between my legs. "My other self was... insistent about trying that one."

"I should have thought about doing it before. I've seen him grow. I just haven't felt it."

Hades chuckled. "He's a greedy bastard. Did you like being treated like a toy?"

With anyone else, I would have said no. But with Hades, the answer was yes. He knew I liked our encounters dark and intense, just like he did, but outside the bedroom (or hallway or forest or cave) he revered me. His subjects worshiped me like they did him. Hades was still making sure his entire Realm knew to do so, but the way he spoke with such conviction about my abilities and worthiness only made me want to give him more.

We looked out at the view. From up here, we could see forest and cloudy night sky. The Far Realm was dangerous, but I loved it. I'd found my powers here. I'd found Hades.

He pressed me back against his body, holding me firmly in place. I trailed my hand through the water.

"How big does he get?" I asked.

"Big enough to split you open."

I hummed.

"Don't get any ideas," Hades warned. "He'll get greedy again."

I laughed. "Probably best not to get bigger than that. I won't be able to sit for a while."

He nuzzled his lightly bearded face against my hair. "Then we'll do all our work lying down this week."

"Sounds tempting, but I can't create the underworld for human spirits if I'm doing that."

For the first time, Hades sounded regretful. "I should have thought of that."

"It's okay." I swished around to face him, laying my palm against his cheek. "I could have said no."

"You didn't know what I—he—was going to do."

"As if I don't know you."

His eyes sparkled back at me. "You like having me so deep inside you can barely breathe?"

I nodded.

He stepped forward, forcing me to back up. "You like it when we both take you at the same time?"

Another nod.

"When we shoot our cum in your mouth?"

Another nod.

"You like it when we stretch you around two cocks at once?"

We hadn't tried that one yet, but I'd secretly wanted to. My heart hammered. "Yes."

My back hit the wall of the pool. Hades pressed himself against me, leaning in hard for a deep kiss. How was I already slippery again?

He kissed his way up to my ear, wrapping a lock of hair around his fist to direct my head. "Tomorrow," he whispered.

"And many times after that, I hope."

His grip on my hair tightened, forcing my head back. He placed his lips to my throat before answering. "As many times as you want, Persephone."

I opened my eyes. Upside down, our savage kingdom stretched to a dark horizon. How I loved it, and how I loved its savage, dark king.

IF YOU LIKED THIS STORY, CHECK OUT *FLOWERS AND THE FAR Realm* (Hades and Persephone's story) or any of the other Deathless Love books in the series. They're interconnected standalones, so you can begin wherever your mood or curiosity takes you!

2

CYTHEREA'S PERFORMANCE

Damon is invited to the palace to get the queen in the mood for her partner, but he has no idea who he'll be performing with.

This original story includes explicit sex, strong language, voyeurism, mention of abuse and murder, a collar, "good boy", face riding, blowjob, sex as performance

Today I'd meet my partner to perform for Queen Cytherea herself.

Despite living in Aphriso my whole life, I'd never seen Cytherea in person. I'd never been inside her palace. And I never dreamed I'd be having performative sex in her bedroom.

Yet, here I was.

"Right over here." A demi-god with light brown hair indicated the staircase as if it were a common thing.

My mouth gaped. Cytherea's palace was as frothy and white as the egg-white foam on top of rich drinks served in the

Eros-suna. I'd thought the island's largest suna was elaborate and beautiful, but it was nothing like this.

As much as I enjoyed the Eros-suna, a summons from the queen meant I had no choice but to comply. Some people were happy for me. It was an honor to be chosen. Obviously, despite Eros's popular cult, Cytherea ruled here. Serving the ancient goddess of beauty and pleasure filled me to the brim with conflicting emotions. I tended toward optimism, though, and leaned hard into that sense of wonder and excitement, rather than the swirling, frightening alternatives.

The curving staircase was pure white, accented in dark red. Sprays of white feathers and jewels covered the banister. Actual white birds and living flowers perched around the room. Openings weren't mere doors, but tall, pointed things that suggested the next room would be even more opulent. I felt like an explorer or a prince.

The demi-god, beautiful himself, led the way. If the path hadn't been so straightforward, I might have lost him as my eyes wandered to all the magnificence around me.

"This is the queen's chamber," he said, flicking a hand toward the most awe-inspiring set of doors yet at the top of the stairs. Everything in this place seemed to rise up and up, ready to pierce the clouds.

The queen's chamber.

I steeled myself to go in, but my guide continued past the carved white double doors to a much smaller room. "Here. You can meet Iris."

I'd been told practically nothing since getting picked after a performance at the suna. Would I be alone, with a partner, with a group? Rumors suggested Queen Cytherea's preferences, but it wasn't as if I could ask her to find out. Now, at least, I had a name: Iris.

"When do"—a bird squawked, interrupting my question—"when do we perform? Will you come get us?" Nerves, which hadn't bubbled up before a performance in years, cartwheeled in my belly.

"The goddess will call."

That wasn't much of an answer. In fact, it wasn't an answer at all.

He pushed open the comparatively modest white and red door to let me in. The room inside smelled like powder and flowers, a little sickly for my taste.

There was no sign of my partner. I assumed it would be a woman, since we were performing for Cytherea and people often wanted to visualize themselves in the action, but I wasn't sure.

The Eros-suna didn't demand partnerships like this unless both parties enthusiastically agreed to go in blind. I'd performed shows there for years, ever since Eros himself came to Card and revitalized the spaces. Before that, people took advantage of his title as demi-god of lust and did terrible things. He changed that. Now his suna were the perfect place for anybody curious about engaging in a variety of sex acts and scenarios under the careful watch of trained followers. I liked it there. I was good at my job.

Good enough to get the attention of one of Cytherea's attendants.

"Where is the person I'm supposed to meet?" I asked.

Without a word, the demi-god led me further into the powder-smelling room, past mirrors and lights that looked like intricate beaded necklaces. The décor became a little more... careless wasn't the word, but it definitely wasn't as breath-taking and perfect as the rest of what I'd seen in the palace. Maybe this was a multi-purpose room, elegant storage...

The room kept going. I mentally retraced my steps back to the entrance. The way was becoming murky.

Finally, the space ended in a hexagonal shape with three doors. The demi-god chose the one in the middle.

Holding the door open, he indicated for me to go inside. "The queen will call when she is ready."

Instead of entering, he shut the door behind me.

For the first time, apprehension overtook my excitement. No one told me I'd return home after this. There was the possibility that Cytherea might keep me like a pet or punish me if she disliked my performance...

I inhaled, letting curiosity take over again. I was in the palace, for gods' sake. I'd been chosen. This could be fun.

Inside was a sort of makeshift bedroom, again with that storage room feeling—if storage rooms were something goddesses had. A large puffy white mattress lay in a corner, topped with white and red blankets. In another corner was a stand with glittery, filmy pieces of fabric hanging off it. A large mirror leaned against one wall, and a cage with an orange mechanical bird hung from the ceiling. It tilted its head jerkily at me when I entered.

The young woman in the center of the room echoed its movement. Unlike the bird, whose eyes were unnervingly black and unblinking, she had beautiful green eyes. She regarded me with a wary expression, not the excitement of a potential partner.

"Iris?" I guessed.

She flipped long dark hair over her shoulder, more to get it out of the way than to be flirtatious. The movement revealed a piercing in her collarbone. "Yes. You're my new partner?"

I didn't care for the way she looked at me. If she didn't

want to have sex with me, she shouldn't have to. "That's what they told me."

"All right."

Iris really was striking. I could see how she was handpicked by the goddess. Despite wearing a soft-looking two-piece top and flowing pants, the beauty of her body was hard to ignore. She had the light skin of many native to Aphriso. Where it peeked out from her clothes, it looked velvety smooth, her body strong and soft at once. And yes, the outfit did nothing to hide her full breasts and round ass. She had an ease in her body too that I found attractive. So attractive, I found myself getting hard.

"If you don't want to do this," I said quickly, "we can take it slow." I wasn't sure if that was true. Cytherea could call for us any second, and we could say nothing against the goddess who was our queen.

"It's not that," she said, her shoulders relaxing.

I took a cautious step forward. It felt awkward to talk so far apart.

"It's... My last partner didn't turn out so well." She pressed her lips together. Dimples flashed in her cheeks and were gone.

I tensed. No one had told me I was a replacement. "What do you mean?"

"You don't want that story," she said, closing the distance between us. Her effortless sexuality warmed my skin. She stopped right in front of me. "You. What's your name?"

She smelled nothing like the powdery scent in the other room. Iris was sweet, like a favorite dessert warming on the stove. My mouth watered.

"Damon."

She stood silently like someone used to patience.

"From the Eros-suna," I added.

"Shh!" She laid a finger against my lips. "Don't tell the queen that!"

Vaguely, I remembered some bad blood between Eros and the queen. In the suna, people rarely dwelled on those rumors. There were so many other, better ways to entertain ourselves there. But it was natural, I guessed, for the queen not to love a cult dedicated to someone else.

"I won't say anything," I said with a half-smile.

Iris let her finger slide off my lip.

"So," I resumed, "anything I should know about this performance? I'm happy to do whatever she wants that you're comfortable with."

She let out a bitter laugh through her nose. "She'll barely be watching. No, she'll watch the beginning, and then we can do whatever we want. She'll be busy with her husband."

Husband? The only consistent partner people talked about with Cytherea was the war-god Ares, who definitely wasn't her husband. We all knew she was married, of course, but no one talked about him or saw him. It was like he was a ghost. "We're supposed to inspire them?" I guessed.

She pointed at me to confirm I was right. She dropped her voice. "She hasn't said it, but I don't think she can't get in the mood without us, and she has to have sex with him sometimes."

"Hmm." That made sense. Enough, anyway, for me to work with. "Okay, so what do you like? Anything you prefer that I do, or anything to avoid?"

She looked at me sharply. Had I said something wrong? "My last partner didn't ask me that."

"Oh, I—"

"His focus was Cytherea. He knew she liked rough sex with Ares, so that's what he did with me."

It was an asshole move not to ask her what she wanted. "Do you like rough sex?"

"Sometimes. I like switching."

"Switching who's dominant. I like that too."

"Good." She swished hair off her shoulder again. This time it seemed a little more intentional.

"Anything you want me not to do? I don't like biting, personally, giving or taking."

"That's fine," she said. "I won't do that. Umm..." She glanced up at the mechanical bird. "Insults. Please don't."

I knew people at the suna who got off at being told they were sluts to be used, but many people found that mean or offensive. "No problem. I don't love insulting people anyway." I tried a smile.

Iris smiled back, just a slight, coy thing, but very pretty.

We were nowhere near comfortable with each other yet, but having her here stripped away those fears from earlier. I had a likable, attractive partner and a command I understood.

"Anything I shouldn't touch?" I asked, because as the minutes went on, I very much looked forward to touching all of her when the time was right.

"No. I like big hands all over me. And before you ask, oral and anal are good too."

My grin widened. "I'm glad."

I appreciated that Iris was so open. I didn't mind coaching people through their first or second public experience, but it got nerve-racking to have to ask questions about everything when they didn't volunteer information. It made me think I'd miss some small detail that would sully the experience for them. Hadn't happened so far—they tended to love when I guided them through.

"When do we get to go?" I asked.

"Oh, probably tonight." She indicated the gauzy items on the rack. "Now that you're here, she'll want to see what you can do."

That uneasy feeling returned. "See what I can do, huh? I know what I can do, but I've never performed for the queen before. Is she expecting something specific at the beginning?"

Iris shook her head. "I don't think so. She just likes to watch. And then she likes to do, obviously." Her eyes fell to the ground as if she just thought of something. "Maybe if you could mix in some praise. Something romantic."

"Oh!" She didn't put forward the suggestion as if she wanted it for herself. There was another reason. "I can do that. Of course." I raised an eyebrow.

She lowered her voice. "Cytherea likes rough sex the most. If she sees you doing something else in our display, then she won't ask for you later."

The truth dawned. "Is that what happened to your last partner?"

"That's what he wanted, I'm sure. Who wouldn't want to sleep with Cytherea? But Ares..."

The pieces fell together. Ares had killed him. "Was he a demi-god or human?" Full gods couldn't die.

"Human, like me."

"And me." The unexpected connection made me smile. Usually demi-gods were the ones chosen for this kind of thing —they were often tall and gorgeous. Plus, they couldn't die of natural causes. They'd stay beautiful forever.

Unless the war-god Ares decided to cut their lives short.

We humans were extra vulnerable to the whims of the deathless.

Iris acknowledged the connection with a nod. "So we should be careful."

To please the goddess but not too much was a scary line to walk. "Agreed."

Despite our predicament, I enjoyed this new sense of camaraderie with Iris. It felt closer to what we should feel before partnering for a show.

"We're allowed to have fun, though, right?" I winked.

She laughed. "You're making me look forward to this."

"Then I'm doing my job."

"Your job is perfor—"

"My job is making this enjoyable for both of us. It's about making you feel good."

The dimple appeared again in her cheek. She tucked her long, straight hair behind her ear. "Okay, Damon. Does that mean my—"

A knock at the door preceded the same demi-god who'd guided me through the halls opening the door. "Get ready as fast as you can. The queen wants to see you now."

My body charged with the familiar excitement of an impending performance. It helped that Iris looked absolutely stunning. She didn't wear much—a low-cut top that was mostly sheer except for gold and silver stitching, and a pair of soft shorts made of white leather that fell just below her ass. When she walked, her bottom peeked out.

After the demi-god told us to get ready, Iris had thrown on her outfit while I wrestled with mine, so I didn't get a chance to see her naked. I doubted it would matter in the moment, since we'd both done similar things before. Showing our bodies was nothing new.

Dressing like this, on the other hand, was new. From some drawer, Iris passed me a series of white leather pieces I couldn't make sense of at first. Most of them were linked together with chains in the same gold and silver thread as the accents on her top. Finally, I figured out that the largest cuff was a collar and the rest of the outfit clasped unevenly around the rest of my body—shoulder, stomach, hip.

"I thought you said she liked things rough," I laughed, feeling a little ridiculous. The piece covering my pelvis had built-in boning to emphasize my erection, real or imagined.

"Doesn't matter who's the dominant one for the shows," she replied, taking me in. At least Iris appreciated what she saw. "I heard of someone walking their male like a pet and whipping him to get him off."

I'd heard of things like that too, but I'd never encountered it at my suna. "Please don't."

She laughed. The transformation to a genuine smile took my breath away. "I won't make any promises." She looked again at my mostly bare body with open appreciation. The feeling was mutual. "Ready?"

I hooked a loose piece of my hair with a finger. It had gotten trapped underneath the collar. "As ready as I'll be. We can take this off later, right?"

"Of course."

The mechanical orange bird seemed to watch us leave.

"You don't have to make eye contact with her," Iris

explained as we walked quickly back through the long, winding room. "We're there for…"

"Ambience?"

She smacked me lightly. "Exactly," she chuckled.

We reached the outer door, the hall, and finally the entrance to Queen Cytherea's personal chamber. Pausing, I looked to Iris. "Should we wait out here or…?"

But I'd hardly finished my question before the door was opened by a naked female attendant. Many of the ruling deathless had nude attendants, but knowing that didn't make it any less surprising. The feeling in the palace was so different from the suna that the sight took me off guard. A comment swelled in my throat before I swallowed it back down.

"The queen anticipates your presence," said the attendant in a dreamy voice. She didn't appear to look at either of us directly, almost as if she were a spirit from another plane entirely.

I followed Iris's lead and entered. Not much changed in the queen's chamber compared to the staircase and main hall—the ceilings were high, extra pillars arched around the room… It was simply the nicest version of what I had seen. At the end of the room, separated by a door, was the most private area of her personal space. The attendant let us in.

I'd seen pictures of Queen Cytherea. Of course I had. She had white skin and long, golden hair, perfectly formed legs and round breasts. I knew all that. But seeing the queen in person, as naked as the attendant, was an experience I wasn't fully prepared for. The goddess of pleasure looked every inch the part.

She sat on the edge of a red-curtained bed separated from the lower area where we stood by a few steps. Inside the curtains, it was too dim to see her husband, assuming he was already there.

"You must learn speed," said Cytherea. Her irritation chilled my bones, but her voice reverberated like the low, melodious crash of ocean waves.

Iris bowed her head. "We will."

I bowed too.

"Damon," Cytherea purred, a sound that ran directly to my balls. "That is your name?"

"Yes, my queen."

"Put on a good show for me." Her eyes fell to the protruding crotch of my costume.

Iris took my hand, snapping me out of my amazement. I turned to look at her as she sidled suggestively up to me. Okay, this I could do. In a more approachable, human way, Iris could rival Cytherea's beauty. I preferred my partner to the goddess —an interesting revelation I didn't have time to consider because Iris's full lips pressed to mine.

Her arms snaked around me, teasing the places where my small clothing didn't cover. Skin to skin. I did the same, gripping the bare ass showing under her leather shorts. She felt good.

Iris kissed down my jaw to the ear facing away from Cytherea. I took quick stock of the room. My eyes had gone immediately to Cytherea when I entered, so I didn't see what kind of space we were working with. I was used to stages or other clear areas to do my work. Here, it was just a bedroom— a very big bedroom, with rugs and a large settee, but nothing like a stage. I should have asked more questions about expectations.

"I hope you have stamina," Iris breathed warm into my ear.

Her sultry voice woke up my blood and set me throbbing.

"We go as long as she does, and she can go a long time."

I spun Iris around and spoke covertly into her ear next. "How long?"

"An hour at least."

Not unheard of for me, but a stretch. I kissed the spot below Iris's ear. "Have you taken something?"

That should have been my first question, but there were several first questions. When I met Iris, the most important seemed to be her preferences. I never wanted to do something my partner wasn't comfortable with. There were teas and pills to prevent pregnancy. The deathless didn't have to worry about that, but humans did. If I was going to last an hour or more, it would help to not worry about coming inside her.

"Yes." She licked a line up my neck.

That, combined with her sweet scent and the press of her breasts against my chest, made me hard enough to really begin. With a low growl, I picked her up. She responded as I'd hoped, wrapping her legs around my waist.

Over her shoulder, I caught a flash of Cytherea, still watching, making no move to retreat to the darkness of her curtained bed to have sex of her own.

The show was slow to begin. The queen probably wanted us to fuck right away. Despite the stakes, Iris and I had to communicate some things to each other, though. Life in the Eros-suna had taught me how important that was. Now that my most crucial questions were answered, I was ready to pleasure the woman in my arms. Her hair brushed softly against the back of my hands.

I was in my element.

How lucky was I?

Lowering to sit on the white settee, I deepened our kiss. Iris's tongue swept into my mouth and I responded, lapping up more of her taste. She was delicious. Her legs bent on either side of my hips as she straddled me. Then she was moving, grinding against my growing hard on.

I tipped my head back to focus on the sensation as she rode me over the costume, letting out a groan. Her movements rocked to a rhythm, but not like someone purely playing pretend. I'd had partners more focused on performing than on pleasure. Iris wanted the feel of my cock rubbing between her legs. I flexed upward to meet her. At the motion, she grabbed my shoulders with her short, sharp nails. A small, desperate sound forced from her throat.

Okay, Iris was definitely someone I could play with.

Flipping her onto her back, I pulled off the white leather bottoms she wore and grabbed one of her long legs to toss it over my shoulder for better access. Unclipping my ridiculous outfit so I could free my pulsing cock, I shoved the falsely protruding dick to the side and pulled out the real one. A thick vein already ran down the side. It was heavy and ready for the slick, wet warmth of Iris's pussy.

When I locked eyes with her, she opened her mouth suggestively. That was all I needed. I was used to more fore-play, but gods knew I didn't need it. Running the head of my cock through her slickness, I grew hazy with lust. Iris was all lush curves and I needed to be inside her. Now.

With a thrust, I pushed inside. Gods, she was perfect. Tight enough to squeeze around me and loose enough to fit without hurting her with my thick length.

"Oh, yes," I muttered, grimacing with pleasure at the feel of her walls flexing around me. I almost called her beautiful before remembering hazily that the queen had to be acknowledged as the most beautiful, always. I pivoted, impressed I could remember anything with Iris wet around me. "Oh, do that again, baby."

She pulsed around me with her inner walls.

I moaned and drove into her deep. Her whimper made me mindless. Holding her leg on my shoulder, I pushed in faster thrusts, slapping my groin against her.

Dimly, I noticed the white shape of Cytherea had vanished. She'd had a good view of us, so of course she was turned on. Who wouldn't be?

Iris's head bounced against the armrest as I fucked her, her expression in ecstasy. The movement made the stitching on her barely-there outfit move out of place, revealing pert brown nipples.

I ran my hand up the front of her shirt to feel them. Her breasts were big and fucking perfect. The nipples slid between my fingers.

"Oh fuck!" I groaned.

Iris got even wetter when I took handfuls of her.

Normally, I'd take off her shirt during a show so others could see, but I realized I didn't have to. There was something sexier somehow about feeling her and being the only one with a good view.

"Yes, baby, keep doing that," Iris begged. Same pet name I'd used. Good. We were on the same page.

I obeyed, kneading her breasts, teasing the sensitive buds, and growing more frantic as I drove between her legs. I felt so hard I hurt. It was the best, most painful sensation. I was addicted. But it wouldn't last with how fucking sexy she was right now.

With a loud exhale, I pulled out. My cock glistened with

her juices. Had to make this last, she'd said. I panted and sat back on my knee. My other foot had never left the floor.

Iris lowered her leg from my shoulder and rose up to kiss me. Her finger hooked beneath my collar. Okay, that was sexy too. Fuck.

With a violent shiver, I felt her hand circle my rock-hard length. "Oh, I'm too..." But I couldn't finish the sentence.

Her nails lightly teased the skin before she began pumping me.

I'd answered too quickly. I couldn't last an hour. What would Cytherea do, and—oh fuck, right there, *fuck!*

"You have to..." I panted.

She slowed. I didn't need full sentences for her to understand how painfully close I was. "Too much for you, good boy?" She gave a sinful smirk.

I couldn't speak. The smell of arousal and that name—fuck, she was good at this. Finally, I said, "Come here."

I picked her up again and switched our positions. I lay on the cushions and placed her on top of me. "Ride my face."

Surprise lit her eyes. "You're sure? I've always wanted to try that."

Her last partner hadn't done it? I didn't know why I was surprised. She said he was the rough, dominant one. Judging from her attitude when we first met, she acted guarded for a variety of reasons.

"Fuck yes. Come here." I palmed her bare hips to coax her forward.

She leaned forward, kissing me instead of sitting on my face. "What if you can't breathe?" she whispered.

"I'll spank you. How about that?" I grinned evilly.

She felt wet straddling my stomach. I'd be a mess after this, my favorite kind.

With a nod, she sat up again and scooched forward until her pussy lined up with my mouth. Gods, she tasted good! So warm and musky sweet and slippery. But when she started grinding, holding onto the armrest above my head for support, I lost my mind. Her flavor filled my mouth as I flicked my tongue and sucked on her, taking sips of air when she rocked backward.

Her high-pitched keen told me she was close. I groaned, the sound vibrating into her.

"Oh!" She pressed down harder, thrusting against my mouth.

I responded, groaning louder and hanging onto her hips.

"Baby, yes!" she cried.

I was running out of air, but this was too good. She was too close.

I inched my face up to find her clit. Sucking hard, I felt her belly and legs shudder. She gasped out a low, straining noise of pleasure as she came.

As soon as the shuddering lessened, I slapped her on the behind. She tumbled off me, breathing hard.

I licked my lips and sat up, heart pounding. She stood in front of me, her back to the big bed. Now, telltale noises came from behind the curtains.

"Take off your shirt," I said.

With a sensual movement of her hips, she obeyed. I actually laughed in anticipation. That body was enough to bring any man to his knees. And Iris liked to play. "Are you going to take yours off too, good boy?"

She leaned forward and caught my collar with a finger again. The heat from her breasts warmed my chest. "Not this, though. I like this."

Damn...

Hard as iron, I removed the rest of the elaborate costume, trying not to tap my cock. Iris watched and narrated.

"Ooh, I like it when you unclip all those hard-to-reach areas. The way your muscles move... mmm... Oh, did you hit your cock there? Was that painful? You look so hard. Like you want to grab me and fuck me with that big thing. I'd like it between my legs. Almost off. Just one more clip to go..."

I'd almost forgotten about Cytherea. This way, she could hear what was happening.

It was already hot enough seeing Iris naked after making her come. Adding her admiration for my body was almost unbearable.

I sprang up from the settee, collar in place, and grabbed her. She squealed in obvious pleasure. Skin against skin was paradise. I reveled in every place we touched, and our hands roved greedily.

A flash of white in the corner of my eye meant Cytherea had peeked out to look at us. Iris dropped to her knees.

I was already so stiff that her motion made me moan before she began.

The first touch of her tongue to my shaft made me hold my muscles taut. I couldn't see straight. I was only ache and need as she palmed and licked me in one long line.

"You gonna open for me?" I managed.

She opened wide, tongue out.

"Is this what you want?" I gripped myself and slapped my cock down on her wet tongue. Good gods, the sensation that buzzed through my body with each slap...

"Mm hm," she answered without closing her mouth.

"Fuck yeah." I gave her tongue a few more slaps before thrusting between her lips. The dripping heat there nearly drowned me. I growled a deep, incoherent noise.

She kept her mouth open and accessible, pulsing her tongue around me. The way her lips stroked me each time I thrust in, and the deep, tight, forbidden throat swallowing me down—I wouldn't last.

Iris was more than good at this. She obviously loved sex as much as I did, making the most of a situation that could have made others hate the job. She'd fit perfectly in the Eros-suna. I'd take her as my regular partner if I could. Because *fuck* she gave a good blowjob and could ride me like a horse and make me harder than a tree trunk with the mere whisper of "good boy."

"That's it, baby," I grunted, holding Iris's dark brown hair in my fist.

Her eyes flashed up to mine. Tears shone from how deep I drove into her mouth, but crinkles in the corners encouraged me to go on. Those green eyes could bury me.

Soft fingers with long nails reached up to cup me and I nearly came. My movements grew frantic as I rocked faster. She sucked the length of me as if I were a treat.

Finally, with a heavy groan, I exploded into her mouth. She swirled her tongue around my cock a few times, teasing me even after she swallowed all my cum. I shivered at her expert touch.

"Fuck, baby," I moaned, helping her to her feet.

"You were so good."

I kissed her. In the momentary silence, I heard Cytherea breathing hard as she rutted with her husband.

"We have to keep going," Iris breathed.

I wouldn't have had it any other way. "You want me to fuck you with my fingers?" I asked loudly enough for our audience to hear.

"I want you to fuck me with your cock, but I'll wait."

The unexpected answer made me laugh again. "You're amazing." Add something romantic, she'd said. "If you want your good boy to do something else while you wait, just tell me. I can't get enough of you." I wasn't sure how romantic that sounded, but I was so turned on that words barely worked in my head, so it was the best I could do.

Plus, I didn't think she'd have to wait long at all.

"How are those fingers of yours?" she asked, placing both hands on the armrest of the white settee and bending over.

Oh, this was my favorite. Especially when she looked back at me with actual expectancy in her eyes as she wiggled her ass.

And what an ass it was—plump and firm. The stuff of wet dreams.

"They're pretty good," I answered.

"I only take excellent."

Another chuckle vibrated through my chest. "You tell me how they are, then."

Taking a knee, I allowed myself a silent moment to admire her from back here. Then, with a soft, searching grip, I worked up from the back of her knees to the apex of her thighs, teasing her. With a kiss to her big curve, I sent my fingers through her wet sex. I'd tasted her, so I knew some of the shape, but this gave me a new angle to learn even more of her landscape.

Instead of narrating this time, she sighed and let her head hang as I explored her, finding the places where she clenched in needy desire and where she ground against me for more friction. Finally, my thumb anchored onto her clit, rubbing in quick circles, while my middle finger plunged inside her. Another, louder sigh fell from her mouth.

"More," demanded a voice like the oceans.

Cytherea was probably talking to her lover, but I was fairly sure she was talking to us too.

Iris moaned. She obviously enjoyed what I was doing, but the moan was fake. I didn't like that. Real erotic noises or nothing—that was my preference, and Eros's.

"Another finger?" I asked, pumping faster.

"Two more, baby."

I should have expected a cheeky answer. Two more, then. I jammed them all in, soaking them as I kept stroking her clit. Her next shuddering sound was real.

"You want to be fucked, don't you?" I asked. "You want to be fucked by a man in a collar."

I knew it wouldn't take long. I was hard again and ready to thrust inside and bounce against that ass.

Her answering whimper had real desperation in it.

I smirked. "All right, baby."

While I stood, she swept her long dark hair forward over her shoulders and held on.

"Good girl. Hang on tight."

Cries of pleasure and wet slaps emerged from the darkness within the bed. My balls tightened.

Taking her hip in one hand and my length in the other, I filled her in one thrust. She arched at the intrusion. Mimicking the noises coming from the goddess's bed, I fucked Iris mercilessly. Her perfect, round ass cushioned every lunge. She was so wet and turned on that her pale back mottled a flushed red.

Soon, I was feral, driving into her with pure need. Those big, hanging breasts needed to be held against her chest. I squeezed them with the adoration I felt for this perfect body. She'd said something about liking big hands on her.

"Yes!" Iris gasped.

My grunts quieted enough to hear what she'd say next.

"Just like that."

She meant the fucking, not the fondling. I could tell by the way she started fucking me back, rocking and meeting my thrusts with hers.

"Oh, you do that and I'm gonna come," I warned, grabbing her hips again for balance.

"Fuck me," she demanded. "Harder."

Harder? I'd been driving deep and fast already. If I went any harder, I'd explode.

"Harder like this?" I hinged back my hips and smacked in.

"No. Savage."

Fuck me, she was serious. With a growl, I obeyed, using her to get myself off. I was already so close. This panting, shaking, pounding sex, straining to reach the edge would break me. Sweat rolled down my neck.

"Yes!" The word pitched to a scream. "More!"

The noises ripping from my throat were inhuman. I was so aroused that my dick hurt. The only thing that mattered was our feral coupling. I grabbed and pulled, and her pussy clenched around me, and I went faster, and fuck, I was coming. I was streaming inside her, pumping her full of my cum. My orgasm was loud. It didn't get quieter because Iris came right after me, squeezing my sensitive cock in waves I could hardly bear.

I pulled out and walked awkwardly to the seat. Iris, heaving in air like I was, slumped beside me.

"I think I see new colors," Iris said, wincing. Her bottom half had to be sore.

"Those fingers were good, though, right?"

She surged up to kiss me. The side of her breast rested

against my chest. It felt good. But, more than that, there was an honesty to the kiss.

I'd given polite post-coital kisses to strangers before. I'd parted amicably from great performance partners with only a smile.

When Iris kissed me, her fingertips traced my jaw. She lingered, deep and sweet. No tongue this time. It felt more like a thankful or loving kiss. I felt unexpectedly moved.

Wrapping my arms around her back, I pulled her closer so we'd be more comfortable. One of her long hairs got in my mouth.

Wow.

She looked at me, and we weren't only scene partners. To her, that was more than mind-blowing sex. Much more. And she looked even more beautiful now than she had in her room. Her hair was mussed, her face flushed, and green eyes bright. I didn't like to think of myself getting romantically involved with performance partners. The Eros-suna welcomed couples, but, to do my work, it was easier if I focused on giving pleasure to whoever I was paired with that day. I was good at it. I was good at separating my emotions when I had to.

But Iris. She was a ride in more senses than one.

"Good boy," she whispered, a flash of vulnerability slashing through the smirking confidence, almost too quick to see. "You're very different."

She didn't elaborate—the goddess could hear—but I understood what she was saying. Her last partner hadn't been this good. Rougher. Maybe didn't care about her pleasure. I was guessing, but her expression was a conversation.

I scooped her up onto my lap. Instantly, I regretted the pressure on my already sensitive dick, but I refused to put her down again.

The queen panted loudly from within the curtains, followed by a chorus of groans.

Our job was done. It certainly felt that way, at least. I was glad I got to hold Iris a minute longer without thinking of some new way to have loud sex with her. The next time we had sex, it should be with no expectations. Nobody watching.

My lips turned down. That scenario sounded like making love—creatively and wildly, but still with the potential of romance attached. Was that what I wanted?

"Disappointed?" Iris teased, drawing a finger down my lips.

"No," I said, nuzzling into her neck. "That was a fucking dream. You are a dream."

Again, the way she held me meant something more than casual. I planted a kiss on the side of her neck. "Should we leave now?" I whispered.

Iris hopped to her feet. "Oh, yes, before they come out." She picked up her clothes without bothering to put them on. I did the same, and we left.

Attendants acted nonchalant when we exited, flushed and naked.

"I like this collar," I confessed under my breath.

She grinned. "I knew it!"

Together, we found our way back to the room with the orange bird, a spot of color that didn't match the rest of the red and white palace.

We hung our outfits on the rack. I met Iris's gaze. "I think I'll keep this on for now."

She looked smug and pleased. "Good. You might want to take it off to wash, though. Then you can put it on again."

"You think Cytherea will call us that soon?"

She rolled her lips as if deciding. "No."

The collar wouldn't be for the queen, but for Iris. She was asking a question.

"Then of course I will," I answered.

I didn't know what the future held, but Iris dragged me lightly forward by the collar until I met her for a soft kiss.

Uncertainty could wait. We were here, now, together. A summons beyond our control had drawn us to the palace. The best we could do was enjoy each moment. And this moment was heaven.

3

SIREN'S SEAT

Patrolling dangerous siren breeding grounds leads Valen to find a lone male, who allows her to fulfill her most unmentionable fantasy.

This original story includes explicit monster sex, strong language, mention of death and harm

"Warmer weather means...?" Orpho prompted. Owl-like feathers coated the face and neck of our commander as he peered at us.

"Less fucking wind?" my friend Carina whispered in my ear.

We were all sick of it. Even inside, we could hear it howl, lashing against the walls of our small outpost. The walls were black and green, nearly camouflaged against the pine forest with its rocky coast beyond.

Most of the dozen or so people in my security detail had worked on the coast of the Far Realm for decades. Every year, there was a period of about two weeks when catastrophic storm winds blew the Stygian Sea into a frenzy. Didn't mean we could stay inside, though. King Hades was serious about security, despite having every kind of dangerous demi-god and creature here in his Realm. That meant heartier beings like us getting recruited.

I snorted a laugh through my nose and craned to see around the people in front of me. My hands itched to reach out with a bit of my power and freeze them in place just long enough for me to see. Why did everybody have to sway like that?

"Siren breeding," muttered a few voices in answer.

"That's right," Orpho confirmed. "Keep everyone away from the shores this week."

I nodded with the others, hooking a thumb in my wide belt. Sirens were dangerous at the best of times. During breeding season, they were murderous. No hunger needed before they'd rip your head off.

"As if anyone's going to the beach," Carina said.

The gale outside gave an answering whistle.

"Maybe they deserve what they get."

"Shut up," I replied. "We've got a job."

Carina was a good friend when I needed one, but her negativity weighed down an already sour day. No one deserved to get murdered by a siren. I was with Hades on that one. That meant I couldn't complain too much about going out into the wet wind.

Orpho didn't bother dismissing us. We all knew what to do. Each of us patrolled overlapping patches of land near the shoreline. With all the different powers represented by the demi-gods here, choosing the right rotation for everybody wasn't easy. But now that we knew where to do, it was like a damn dance.

My spot? Right along the water.

If a siren saw me, I could freeze their movement just long enough to escape. Carina, with her ability to see one layer beyond the usual plane of sight, couldn't help with that. So she was stationed inland. Lots of trees and obstacles there.

"Mad that you're gonna get eaten by a siren?" Carina asked as we moved toward the heavy, metal-reinforced door.

More than sirens lived out there. This wasn't a job for cowards. Since I started doing this a few decades ago, we'd lost scores of people in every horrific way imaginable. The first few years, I thought a lot about what I'd grown up wanting to do— move to Nalia. Buy a boat.

I didn't confess it to anybody, but mermaids fascinated me. None of those here in the Far Realm. Only sirens, who had some similar traits. Enough of them, honestly, that I'd read about them in my spare time.

Okay, more than read.

Studied.

Drew.

Made charts.

Took extra trips to the shore to try to see them.

Fantasized.

Obsessed.

Siren breeding season was the most dangerous time for anyone wandering near their territory, but that didn't mean I would stay away. I wanted to watch.

Male sirens were hugely illusive. I'd never seen one in person. Female sirens, yes. On many occasions. Mostly from afar.

Male sirens, according to every source I'd managed to scrounge, resembled merpeople in almost every way. They didn't have the same predatory fangs as their female counterparts. Often, they'd get savaged by their mates during or after breeding. To avoid that, they'd developed an extra penis to please the female. There wasn't enough research on that topic, and it was difficult to find more without giving my bizarre obsession away. But I was convinced that nothing, *nothing*, was sexier than a male siren breeding. The desperation they felt when holding the female in place, biologically compelled toward sex but terrified that she would tear him apart...

I swallowed. Moisture already gathered between my legs. I looked at Carina. Not even she knew my filthy fantasy of getting fucked by an impossible-to-find male siren.

Someone ahead of us opened the door. Cold wind whipped my short hair around my face, even though I'd tried to tie it back.

"At least that would be a memorable way to go," I replied.

THE COAST OF THE FAR REALM WAS PICTURESQUE ON GOOD days. This wasn't one. Churning water and wind made it difficult to see more than few steps ahead.

Being able to freeze someone else's movement was only helpful if I could see them coming. The night had me on edge. It wasn't an unusual night—siren breeding season arrived every year. The wildness in the air probably stirred up those irresistible primal urges to mate.

I closed my fist around the mid-length knife at my waist. All security patrols here had a variety of tools, but that was the most versatile. The rope, spyglass, and bursting pebbles (meant to disorient) would do shit in this weather.

Sirens bred slightly north of my location. At least, coupling hadn't been recorded in this area that I'd ever found. And I'd looked.

The rest of the year, I kept my hobby to off hours. During my shift, I focused. Had to, especially as a shorter female. Despite my stocky build, my short-for-deathless stature meant extra danger in certain situations. When I focused, I could handle myself. Even enjoyed the work. But when I went home, thoughts of sirens and mermaids seeped in again, inevitable as the familiar scent of my little house. I liked their biology, the legends... all of it. No fact or rumor was too small.

These two weeks kept me on edge. The weather made me feel wilder too. The idea of encountering a siren buzzed along my skin, both the threat and arousal of it.

I wasn't myself today.

"Fucking mud," I grumbled, lifting one boot out with a sucking sound that rose even above the wind.

No deathless being, human, or creature appeared, unless I counted the silver snakes and fish that sometimes glistened in the waves between sheets of rain. Just up the slope from the wet sand and muddy reeds lived a settlement of fauns. They'd be dinner in a second if a siren caught them spying. Little chance of one coming down this far, but it was possible. Enough danger existed that I had to clear this long stretch of beach before trekking up to the settlement and patrolling to make sure everyone knew not to go beyond the boundaries of their little village.

Last year, a little one had drowned. It wasn't during my shift, but I still felt responsible, like I should have done something.

On days like these, I needed jolts of inspiration every couple minutes to keep me on task. Otherwise, I'd get miserable enough to consider quitting. My uncle lived in Nyx, the biggest city. We'd been close once, but we hadn't spoken in years. I couldn't count on his charity if I gave up this job.

What was I thinking? Charity? Was I fucking kidding myself?

It was just the weather and the sirens getting to me. I'd make it through. I always did. And then I'd remember why I liked this job most of the time, even when it was dark and bloody and tedious and terrifying.

A building appeared through the sheets of rain, mounted on huge stones to avoid the worst of the waves. Whoever built that had never seen the Far Realm this time of year. Water surged against it, receded, and surged again.

Good thing it was abandoned. It used to be a house, then a sailor's outpost, then a research station, then nothing. Children played there sometimes. People probably used it for a secret fuck sometimes too.

Someone could be in there. The waves crashed against the open part underneath, but I knew the bottom section beneath the main building had been carved out deeper than it looked from the outside. The storm probably hadn't drowned everything.

I sheathed my knife before cupping my mouth. "Anybody here?"

No one answered. But I heard an extra noise. It wasn't rain or wind or waves. I knew every variation those sounds could make. This was a slap.

Somebody or something was inside.

"Shit." I grabbed the knife again and looked for a way in. Nobody should have been inside the building. It was siren season, for fuck's sake. Not to mention the raging storm.

Wetness poured down my face. I rubbed my eyes to see more clearly.

A wave gushed beneath the elevated structure and subsided.

Another slapping sound.

Cursing, I ran in, racing the next onslaught of water. *I should have enough time to—*

A roar rumbled as another salty wave hit the building and flooded up to my ankles. Chest heaving in the darkness, I trotted a few more steps uphill. Sand became a rocky cave set into the hill. I'd passed the part with the building on top. Here, the noise of the storm muted to a shush. Even without rain and wind in my eyes, it was difficult to see. Shadows pierced every corner of the hollow space.

I squeezed my eyes in a blink to clear them and adjust. More came into focus.

Good. I was starting to think I'd done something monumentally stupid by running in here blind.

A figure outlined against the dark. Lying down. Hurt, maybe?

My heartbeat kicked up. "You need to go home now. It isn't safe. I'm here for security." I thumbed a magicked light from my belt. It was round and gave enough illumination to shine for about an hour. For emergencies only. I always overused mine. (Why the hell not? I figured. The two demi-gods who could add more light to them took maybe a minute on each one. Better to see.)

The figure didn't respond to me. Instead, the wide eyes of a cornered animal looked back into mine.

No, not an animal. The face was almost human, male, with kelp-green hair growing past his shoulders. He lay on his side, hard, defined muscles flowing over his broad chest to a tapered waist. Skin gave way to luminous green-blue scales. His thick, long tail was drawn up, almost where knees would have been. Another slap sounded as the end of his tail thrashed nervously.

The siren's lips parted in terror. Apart from the massive tail, he didn't move.

I hadn't frozen him in place. But I felt frozen myself.

What in Abaddon's god prison had sent a male siren here?

He was a beautiful specimen. Person, not specimen. And... here.

I took a step forward.

The siren held out a hand. "Don't." The one word came out heavily accented.

Male sirens used a different language than female sirens, who usually lived in groups on the shore. Males were solitary sea-dwellers. I was surprised to hear the common tongue at all.

"Why are you here?" I asked.

It could have been the wrong question, but at least I asked a coherent one. This felt like all my fantasies come to life. I could drink in the sight him and always want more. He was fucking gorgeous. And obviously nervous.

I needed to check my cravings and make sure he was safe. Heart throbbing, I showed him my knife and put it away so he would know I wasn't a threat. Only female sirens killed demi-gods. He probably wouldn't hurt me. But then again, the research and even wild stories about male sirens were slim.

The light from the emergency globe in my hand shone on his skin. I knew siren skin ranged in tone, but I honestly couldn't tell what color his was. Grayish silver? Green? Light brown? Maybe all three.

"It's safer here," he said slowly, suddenly squinting as if to brace himself.

Was he in pain? "Are you all right?"

When he opened his eyes, the light and sadness in them were regal. My stomach flipped. "I promised I would not go. My brother died."

I nodded. His brother was killed while breeding. "How can you stop yourself?"

Shit. That was a personal question. I'm asking personal questions to a siren.

Breeding was supposed to be such a primal instinct that males traveled yearly to the beach, even though a few of them died every season.

He winced again. I hated myself for it, but watching the way his chest and stomach constricted with the movement made me wet for a different reason than the rain.

"I promised. I will try."

"Are you planning to stay here for two weeks?" I asked, skeptical.

Hopelessness colored his expression.

"I... I didn't mean..." Since when did I blather like this? I rallied. "You can't stay here. It's too dangerous for the children who live up the hill."

His brow lowered. "Dangerous?"

"Yes, this time of year." Even male sirens became dangerous for different reasons during breeding season. His glorious tail drawn up like that? It meant he was ready to mate. Female sirens chose mates largely based on the size of their tails when the males created a seat for them. After they inspected the males, they chose the most impressive one by coming close enough to grab. Males pinned the female to their seat and the process began.

"You know about sirens?" he asked, but he didn't use the word *siren*. It was a more musical sound. And yes, I knew what it meant. Hearing him say it just twisted my heart more. I'd never been this close to exactly what I wanted.

I eyed his seat, the place where skin became scales and bent upward, like a backrest.

"Yes," I admitted. "I know a lot about sirens. I'm here making sure no one gets hurt."

"If I leave, I will get hurt."

"I know." I took another step forward. "You might." I plowed forward, knowing I'd regret this either way, whether I said it or not. "But I'm sure you'd get chosen with a tail like that."

Obviously pleased, the siren slapped the end of his tail again. The apprehension and sadness I'd seen in his eyes turned into something hungrier as I took another small step forward.

Then shock crossed his features, as if he realized something. "Stop."

The way he said the one word was yummy enough to eat. Desire moaned in my chest. But I stopped.

"You know about sirens," he continued. "You know what will happen if you come too close."

I did know about sirens. I knew he'd grab me. I also knew that only one sexual encounter satisfied the urges that drew male sirens to breeding grounds in the first place.

That meant, he could return to the sea if we...

I chuckled, not believing I could be so vile.

The siren looked confused.

"That's true," I said. "I do know. And I also know you have to leave."

"I will not eat you. Or anyone else."

I laughed harder. "I know."

An awkward pause stretched between us.

He broke the silence. "I must stay." His full lips twitched. "For as long as I can."

The air felt thicker between us. Outside, the storm rushed. "Can you go back to the sea?" I asked softly.

He moved green hair back over his shoulder. "No." Instinct was nearly impossible to break, even harder than my addiction to sirens. I wouldn't argue with him.

I changed my question. "When can you return to the sea?"

"Once the heat is gone, or if I break my vow and survive."

Two agonizing weeks fighting his very biology or once he got to mate.

Don't say it. Don't suggest it. Breeding with sirens wasn't expressly forbidden or anything, but it didn't have to be. For a million reasons, no one fucked a siren. But how many people had been alone in a sea cave with a non-predatory member of the species?

I evaluated him. He was very large, from his muscular tail to his sheer size and physique. Freezing his motion would do nothing to help me get him out of here. I didn't want to threaten him. To me, what he wanted felt fair. He didn't want to get eaten during sex. Who could blame him?

I could tell the fauns in the village not to come down here. But then, I couldn't control what they did. That one young faun last year was proof of that. If I confessed the reason— that there was a male siren in here—curiosity would absolutely get somebody in trouble.

"I don't want to punish you," I said, stalling until I thought of a plan.

Apprehension widened his eyes again. "Please."

I couldn't believe I was actually entertaining the idea of indulging my most secret craving. But he was so beautiful, and it could actually *help*. The world was a crazy and messed up place, but this situation was possibly the craziest.

If this actually happened, this fantasy in my head, I'd offer sacrifices to the Divine.

"What if," I began, "you could go back to the sea today?"

"I can't." Desperation shone in his face. He was pleading with me. Gods, how I wanted him...

"You said you would have to wait or break your vow. I don't want you to have to do either. What if there was another way?"

He breathed heavily, his chest rising and falling with nerves and confusion.

"What if I got close to you?"

There it was. My secret was out. I was so twisted.

Then I remembered the power dynamic here. I should have seen it before, but I was on security patrol, the siren was powerless, and I'd just proposed fucking him.

"It's not a command," I said in a rush. "Only an option. I know that once you... if we... then you could return to the sea. I've heard."

Gods, I sounded like an idiot.

"You would not hurt me?"

His question broke my heart. He probably watched his brother get attacked and killed by his mate. He'd surely seen that happen to others.

"No. I won't hurt you, I promise. What's your name?"

"I am called Elu."

"Valen."

His answering look pooled warmth in my belly. He was starting to believe me, starting to consider this delicious new solution.

I wasn't traditionally beautiful myself, so I'd never thought a being this luminously stunning would ever look at me like *that*. With hunger. With desire. With an appetite so ravenous it would risk death.

I decided.

"I want to step closer," I said, removing my belt of weapons and tools. Another show of good faith.

"Come."

That one word sent vibrations through my entire body. Elu the siren wanted to snatch me with that muscled arm and pin me to his seat.

Trembling with excitement—*control yourself, it's happening, it's happening!*—I removed my muddy boots and pants. It took too long. My mind swirled around everything I knew about sirens and about this moment.

He wanted it. I wanted it.

Fuck fuck fuck.

I couldn't think beyond the molten need consuming my body.

Naked from the waist down, I stepped over the cold, wet stone toward Elu.

A flash of intensity lit his eyes the second before he lashed out and captured my wrist, like a predator catching fish. His fingers felt cold, smooth, and strong. This close to him, it was easier to see the musculature of his arms, his neck, the beauty of his angular face... all the exquisite detail I'd only imagined in my dreams. I drank in every detail.

He yanked me forward and grabbed my leg with the other arm. My own instinct had me reaching for the belt that wasn't there. I didn't let others manhandle me. But this? I'd do this every day for the rest of my life.

Elu expertly forced me into place, straddling him, leaning

against his massive tail. His movements were quick, rough, even frenzied.

Open like this on top of him, my sex already throbbed. I tried to take in the moment, but I almost felt outside my own body. My mind raced too far ahead.

Male sirens have no visible genitalia. It protrudes during breeding.

Demi-goddesses didn't have to worry about pregnancy like humans or sirens did, thank the Divine. Elu would come inside me. He'd come inside me.

Oh gods.

Heat flooded my face and my chest. I was actually sitting on a siren's seat. Elu's large hands positioned me before holding me in place, pressing me down against his cool skin. His forearms pressed against my thighs and fingers dug into my sides. Between my legs, his muscles moved.

I gasped as something tickled, almost swimming as it entered me.

I knew about this. I dreamed about this. Male sirens pressed their mates down against their seat, which opened up the hidden slit hiding their first cock (yes, first). It grew fast, swimming up like an eel deep into the female.

It felt strange. I released a strangled sigh as he went deeper and deeper.

Elu didn't thrust as he watched my face. Sirens' bodies moved for them, gaining speed and intensity as the arousal peaked.

I didn't want him to fear, so I set down the light and raised my arms to grip his tail near my head. He shivered. Hopefully that was a good shiver.

He was long, deep, and now he was hardening. Elu's eyes blazed. For sirens, this was the most dangerous part, when they became locked together.

I groaned. His cock was already so deep, and it was thickening, filling me completely, stretching my walls. Fuck, I loved it. I flexed around him and he shuddered. His grip on my waist tightened.

When would he stop growing, getting harder? Fuck, he was wedged so far inside... Was this a bad idea?

I whimpered, trying to make room, but he wouldn't let me move. When I opened my eyes, Elu's intensity had heightened. He had the face of a madman, someone desperate to finish.

When his cock punched up inside me, my whole body jolted. Elu's taut muscles didn't move except to keep me steady. On its own, his long dick fucked me hard.

I growled and clung to Elu's huge tail, riding waves of sensation that left me a sopping, slippery mess.

His thick cock pumped so hard it almost hurt. If I moved—

"Fuck!"

Pleasure like I'd never known coursed between my legs, spreading to my whole body. I was shaking, begging, a trembling disaster of pure need.

The second cock. Small, hard, emerging at the height of his arousal to vibrate against my clit. It was perfect.

No wonder some females stopped feeling murderous and came hard enough to unleash the male's orgasm too. No fucking wonder.

My pleading turned into writhing, but I had nowhere to go. Elu held me in place with the determination of fear. He couldn't come until I did.

He teased and rubbed my clit while he pounded hard into me. All that, while staring into my eyes with courage, of all things.

I sobbed, seeking release. This much pleasure was almost pain.

Both his hard-ons grew more frantic, tearing release from me by force. My cry was almost a scream. It echoed off the walls. I drenched his cocks in my cum.

At that instant, he groaned loudly, the first noise he'd made the whole time, and filled me with jets of warmth. He panted, showing off those distinct swimming muscles.

Then he shoved me off him and backed away.

I nearly fell. It wasn't as if my legs were working. I could barely think a full sentence.

"What?" I began. Then remembered.

Siren mating was lethal to many male sirens. Even if they survived sex, they might be killed right afterward.

I understood why he moved away so quickly, but I missed leaning against his tail, hearing his fin smack the rock. I missed his enormous cock inside me.

I was just with a siren. A siren. Gods, I was still so turned on.

He looked at me, bracing two hands on the stone floor. His hair fell over his rounded shoulder.

"I'm still not going to hurt you," I said.

He blinked a couple times, as if digesting that information. His dicks were still partially out, retracting back beneath his skin.

"I believe you."

His quiet confession rose above the whipping wind outside. I'd won the trust of a male siren. That was one of the greatest accomplishments of my life.

We stayed still in each other's presence for several long moments before he said, "I return every year."

"I'll meet you here, Elu."

He smiled, unearthly in his beauty and strangeness, and returned to the sea.

❧ 4 ❧

SECOND RITUAL

On Juniper's second visit to her boyfriend's vampire clan, she participates in another full moon ritual, where the vampires release their feral sexual energy.

Inspired by Luca and Juniper's story in *Full Moons and Vampires*, this story includes explicit sex, strong language, a MFMM situation, orgy, mention of blood

The second time I went to Sosnakrev, Luca let me bring my notebook. Of course, I'd brought it the first time too, but I hadn't written down anything specific about the full moon ritual, per my promise. Vampires had kept it secret for hundreds of years. I wasn't about to ruin that tradition.

This time, though, I could make notations just for us. Research made me come alive. Because of that, I convinced Luca that a few small notes would help me relive the intense experience at home. I could look at the dots to signify the exact location of the blood cisterns, or the squares to show where the sacrifice platforms were, or a few of the words the older female vampires said before giving us a pill and telling us where to put our clothes, and it would all come rushing back.

"Bare yourself to the moon." Lines fanned from the older vampire's eyes as she looked at me. Her suspicious expression showed she only half-remembered a faun participating in the moon ritual a few months ago, where Luca had claimed me as his own. He was probably already in the darkened hollow now. Judging from his violent need last night, he would not feel patient as he waited for me among the other members of his clan.

I removed my clothes and handed them to an attendant. My throat felt a little scratchy from swallowing the pill dry, but it was a must. Without it, any number of vampires could impregnate me. Fauns and vampires weren't like the deathless that way, able to control their own body's time.

But that was a fascinating subject for another day.

Today was the moon ritual.

I stepped through the pavilion with its open walls to overlook the clearing below. Above the pines, the moon was rising, piercing bright. A kernel of old apprehension bloomed in my chest. After two years of dating a vampire who would say nothing about this wild monthly orgy with his clan, full moons made me tense. Luca didn't like what the moon did to him. He slowly morphed from being a sweet and conscientious chef at one of the inns with so-called "demon rooms" to someone more savage, more greedy.

As much as I adored having sex with his normal, kind side, I preferred him feral when he loosened up enough to allow it. Right before we left on this trip, I'd had to wear a scarf to my work at the Assembly of Nyx to cover up bruises. Luca hated that he hurt me in the mad scramble to take all he could from my body. I knew he was nothing like the blood-sucking monsters some creatures still thought vampires to be. But if I could have him desperate, I'd take him that way any time. I had enough scarves. Chilly weather in the Far Realm meant I often wore long sleeves and bottoms anyway.

Speaking of chilly, tonight was growing chilly too. We weren't out of the winter season, a busy time for me at work. When I heard it was a good month for me to visit, though—Luca's turn at the ritual, enough time off for both of us—I jumped at the chance.

Wrapping my arms around myself, I peered down into the hollow. The dark figures of vampires clustered like snarling creatures. Their bat-like wings flapped and furled. In the dark, I could still see them easily because of their pale skin. But where was Luca?

My eyes skimmed over the heads of the stalking bodies. I stepped carefully down the path. Last time, I hadn't needed to walk this way. I'd gone from one of the high platforms off to the left above the hollow, to careening down in Luca's arms.

A female vampire passed, bumping into me as she went. Moon energy didn't make anyone polite.

I picked up my pace. I was in my head again. I paused my search for Luca—he'd find me any second—and noticed details I'd missed the first time. There were the cisterns, the drums, the newer vampires posted on the lip of the hollow, handing out brushes, cups, and... were those stakes? Emergency purposes, I guessed, but it was odd.

I lifted my folded arms so they covered my hard-nippled breasts. Even with everyone else naked too, it felt weird to stroll into a hollow full of unbelievably gorgeous vampires as a short, curvy faun wearing nothing but the hair on her head.

So many people looked at me, not as they would look at a

stranger, or as an unexpected addition to a meeting (I'd seen that look too many times to count.) They stared like they were waiting for a signal to strike. It was a look predators got before going in for the kill.

Where was Luca? Too bad I wasn't taller.

When the drumming and chanting started, I actually breathed a sigh of relief. The beginning of the ritual would steal some attention away from me and let me find my boyfriend. Plus, the idea of starting made me squirm with anticipation. The last time had been explosive enough to cement me and Luca together as perfect mates. Could anything live up to that first time?

He wasn't here. I tried my luck, worming through gaps in the crowd and earning only fangs bared in lust or anger. Or both, definitely both.

The drumming grew more frantic. The ritual couldn't start without Luca by my side. I opened my mouth to call his name but thought better of it. No one here did things like that. There were mates, and then there was us. Luca wanted to be by my side the whole time.

The air smelled like sex before we even began. That, and cold grass, which had a smell I could never name.

The drumming stopped.

Oh no.

A hand closed tight over my wrist. Luca pulled me to him a second before the chaos of the ritual erupted.

"Luca!" I gasped.

"Jun." His voice was an angry, desperate rasp. "I could smell you from the second you entered." Fangs showed above his lip as he took me in. He always kept those tucked away, but the moon madness was on him.

I'd been so busy observing and looking for him that I

hadn't gotten properly excited. Seeing him now, though, his pale skin flushed in the moonlight, pupils blown wide, expressive face full of ferocious need for me, my belly twisted. Lust heated my cool skin.

Behind me, someone licked my spine.

Luca snatched me away, possessive. Vampires ran cold, so they rarely sweated. I, on the other hand, sweated pretty often. Luca loved it. And so did all the other vampires in his clan.

The one behind me persisted. I glanced back. A beautiful female with long black hair, almost blue in the moonlight.

Luca dropped to his knees, diving between my legs. I gave a little gasp and rested my hand on his head. His tucked wings flared out, shook. While he explored me, I ran my hand along the rigid top edge of one wing. Luca growled, which felt amazing. Hopefully he'd do it again.

What was I saying? We had all night.

Last time, I'd felt as wrung out as a used rag by the end, pushed and pulled and speared by so many vampires I hardly knew which end was up. Luca was my only constant. He was with me, or looking at me. We'd check in on each other.

I reminded myself to relax, not be so analytical. It was hard to let go of that part of me, since I used it every day during work and at home.

I'm with Luca, my perfect mate. And he's literally between my legs right now. I'm in a crowd of naked, horny vampires.

My breathing changed as I sank into the sensation of his mouth. Once he transported me far enough, I liked the voyeurism and group sex. But I was still new to it.

"Luca," I moaned.

Another vampire joined us from the side, this one a female also. She ran a cool hand up my body, pressing against the length of my side. Her fingers teased my breasts wonderingly. I didn't remember her from last time. She made her way to my throat and directed my head to kiss her. I did, matching the movements of my tongue to Luca's.

Okay, yes, I loved this.

Luca gripped my legs, rotating them slightly so he could get a better angle. I sucked in a breath. He licked savagely at my clit, and I clenched, breaking away from the one I was kissing.

"Oh my gods," I whimpered. My legs shook.

With a shove, Luca pushed me down. I wobbled, afraid I'd fall on the hard ground, but instead I found skin. Someone else behind me rutting into their partner. I sat on his moving back. The new sensation as Luca sucked me brought me close to the edge.

Moaning and pinching me with his fangs, Luca got on his hands and knees. I struggled to hold on.

Around us, acolytes brought blood and water to whoever wanted it. They were the only ones who were silent. The rest of the field shouted or cursed or groaned. The hollow crawled with desperate, feral life.

A male vampire, maybe around Luca's age, broader, sidled behind him. His dick already glistened in the pale light. How long had the ritual been going on? It didn't seem like very long.

He grabbed Luca's hips and I watched, oddly mesmerized, as he began fucking him from behind. The new motion only made my pussy wetter. Luca's head bobbed against me as he lapped me up, targeting that spot I liked and grinding his tongue against it in a circle.

My body seized. I didn't know how to move as I came. I twisted, shuddering violently, with a hoarse sound.

Luca rose, mouth wet, and hoisted me up. I stole a kiss as he gripped my leg and, still pulsing back and forth from being fucked, jammed his thick cock into me. It was like having sex with the vampire behind him too. His savage thrusts turned into Luca's ruthless rhythm.

Right when I thought my legs might give out, another male joined behind me. *Oh fuck.* He licked the nape of my neck where my curly hair had parted.

Salty sweat drew vampires almost as much as blood. Especially since they weren't supposed to suck people dry, and they didn't. Despite the full moon ritual putting all their most primal desires on display, vampires had a lot of self-control.

Which they abandoned one night a month with the clan.

The others didn't pause, panting and grunting as they pounded against each other into me. For the third, I was a moving target. My mouth ratcheted open in pain-pleasure as the vampire behind me fit himself in my ass. He was wet too, thank goodness.

When I could open my eyes, Luca met them. It was the first real Luca look I'd gotten tonight. The amusement and arousal there made my heart skip. His sensual mouth curled up. I knew he felt how I'd grown wetter.

I loved being bad with him.

I loved being his.

The four of us clashed and strained and took together. We fell out of sync quickly, chasing our own release. Hands moved from me to Luca. They were everywhere, grabbing what they wanted. I could tell from Luca's slack face that he was dangerously close. And then, yes, he tensed and pumped hard into me, taking handfuls of my hips (one of his favorite features about me, he said once.)

The one behind Luca came almost at the same time. Heaving heavy breaths, he lumbered off to fuck someone else. They were all so beautiful—the males, the females... Luca was my favorite, but vampires were sexy. There was no other word.

The vampire behind me slid out at some point and moved on.

Luca and I joined and separated, caught in a frenzy of lust. We drank water. I rode him while he sucked someone else off. For a while we even flew and fucked in the air, like that first time. Moon energy didn't steal my mind as completely as it did the vampires, but there was nothing like the full moon ritual. So many lovely bodies pressing and straining around us. Luca was mine, so I didn't need to feel jealous or possessive. He would always be mine. At the end, I was left a tired, panting mess.

As the sky began to lighten, Luca and I lay on the ground and laughed. It was ridiculous, having sex with all these people at once. I could never write down what just happened, even for research. But there was nothing like it. On paper, it would sound crass—the most intimate secret shouted to a world that couldn't understand. But Luca and I understood.

Too bad more fauns didn't date vampires. They had no idea what they were missing.

IF YOU LIKED THIS STORY, CHECK OUT *FULL MOONS AND VAMPIRES* or any of the other Deathless Love books in the series. They're interconnected standalones, so you can begin wherever your mood or curiosity takes you!

WILDNESS CLUB

A human woman joins the Wildness Club for the day. Will her dream of joining the god of the hunt—as the hunted—come true?

This original story includes explicit sex, strong language, feral play, sex club, shifters

I tightened the strings of my mask. The stiff black lace covered not only my eyes but my entire face. It made me nervous to wear such a precious item out on the streets, so here I was in front of Orion's manor, still fiddling with my disguise.

Would they let me in if they knew who I was?

Orion, god of the hunt, had a whispered reputation—one ripe for gossip, but not bad enough to stop. Veiled jealousy colored many of the comments about his illusive club. Most weren't allowed inside his manor at all. He was famously secretive. Being broad and handsome (allegedly) let him get away with more than humans would be allowed to do in Kantharos. At least, that was my theory.

Dusk made the air balmy. This was my favorite time of day, when fireflies twinkled and adventure sparkled in corners. A time for wildness.

Satisfied that my mask wouldn't slip, I knocked on the huge wooden double doors. They thundered so loudly that my heart skipped.

Shit. This was supposed to be a secret club, not a party where anyone could knock and get in.

I swallowed, skin crawling. Lights peeked from high windows. There were none on the ground floor.

This was a bad idea. Coming here alone made me prey for greedy gods or thieves. Just getting to Orion's manor had been an ordeal, and it wasn't as if I'd been invited.

Orion's province lay to the north, where tame, comfortable towns gave way to a wilder landscape overgrown with forests, lakes, and meadows. In the center of it all rose the manor, with turrets of river stone and smooth wooden statues of hawks and stags protruding from second-floor balconies. Rustic, wild elegance.

No one answered the resounding knock.

Biting my lip, I pressed my ear to the door. Impulsive. Silly. But I could hear murmured voices and glassware clinking and a woodwind playing a haunting, upbeat melody.

How long should I wait? What I'd heard about a party was true—thank the gods—but no one seemed interested in inviting me in.

My mind traveled back down the long path I'd walked to get here. It would take even longer getting back, since I tired myself out on the journey. I should have taken the stableman's offer of a horse. But no, I didn't want to sully my slinky black dress with horse hair.

If I weren't so desperate for a change, I never would have come this far at all. A minimum of two nights at an inn two hours' walk away (if I couldn't get an invitation to the manor) and then the inevitable questions when I returned home.

I told the staff I was visiting a friend, since I had to account for my every movement, even now at twenty-seven. As the next Vesta-kori (okay, second in line—my mother still hadn't taken over for my grandmother) I had to be proper, polite, diplomatic, a symbol of hearth and home in the goddess's stead. I'd be a beast not to be grateful for tea and lemon cake and demi-god servants to tend the palace. But I longed for freedom too, even if only for a night.

"You've arrived at a strange time, my lady."

I spun to the face the owner of the rich voice. *My lady.* Did he know who I was? My pulse kicked up.

And not only from surprise.

A man—god, by the look of him—stepped out from trees and bushes on the side of the path leading to the manor. He wore a black suit with a black mask similar to mine. None of that could hide the thick muscles that bulged beneath the fabric or the square jaw framing a large, brutishly handsome face. He appeared completely at home, as if it were the most natural thing in the world that he should emerge from the trees like a bear or other creature.

"I know I'm late," I said.

I didn't know that at all—I'd only guessed when to arrive, and then walking all that way took longer than I'd expected. My feet throbbed.

The stranger approached with long strides. "Very fine lace," he observed.

To my horror, he reached out to touch the edge of my mask. I reeled back. "Yes." I covered up my fright with a giggle. "I heard the club only allowed the best, so that's what I brought."

My breath still came short, but I'd recovered enough to look the stranger in the eye. He didn't smile, but his eyes sparkled with amusement through the cutouts in the elaborate disguise. He was broad and well-formed and exactly the kind of person I'd come here to see.

Silence stretched on. I got the sense this man was used to silence.

"May I come in?" As soon as I asked, I realized he could have been another guest coming to the party who had no power to allow me entrance. But somehow, I knew he wasn't. This man either owned the house or had connections strong enough to allow anyone inside that he wished.

"That depends," he answered.

"On what?" I'd brought some money in a bag at my side, but not enough for a good bribe or high fee if he required one.

"On why you're here." One corner of his mouth dimpled as if he chewed the inside.

"I'm here for the club."

"Say its name."

"The Wildness Club."

His eyes fell to take me in. I'd left a generous swath of cleavage visible in my plunging neckline. The fabric fell to my ankles, but it caressed every curve. Compared to the stranger, I was short—another clue that he was a god besides his preter-natural good looks.

"We are very careful about membership," he said. There was no deathless versus human condescension in his tone, only fact.

"How so?"

"There's a trial period when you are assessed." He drew closer.

"Assessed how?" I flushed. In ordinary life, I felt confident in my looks. I was the picture of human femininity in Kantharos: long black hair, bronze skin, enough coquettish curves to fill in a dress. I also had brown freckles and knobby, worker's hands. They were features that didn't bother me normally. Everyone had the bodily detail they wished others not to look at. I felt like this strong stranger might reject me for my inelegant hands. Damn him if he turned me away for something so small.

"We accept only willing members. No curious eyes prying into Orion's business."

"I see." No need to get self-conscious over nothing.

"Do you want to participate?" he asked slowly, raising his hand again.

It felt like a test this time. I couldn't let him take it off and find out I was the granddaughter of the human queen, but I had to let him touch me before he'd allow me inside. It was a matter of trust. Absurd, considering we'd met two minutes ago, and he had prowled out of the leaves like an animal on the hunt.

I stood my ground. He had enormous hands, the fingertips soft and rasping at once as they traced my jaw. If he flipped his wrist forward, he could peel off my expensive disguise with ease. Goosebumps rose where he touched. The scent of fresh-hewn cedar wafted off him through the dark air. Its heady aroma made me lightheaded.

"Yes," I breathed. The syllable came out much more erotic than I expected, as if my yes were a yes to anything this man wanted to do to me.

He dropped his hand. Disappointment flooded my chest at his sudden lack of interest. For a second, I felt like he'd enjoy nothing more than claiming me right here. Was I not enough for him?

Another look confirmed he could have anyone he wanted. I was new. I was late. And I had to prove myself.

With the ease of an owner, he pushed open the door to admit us both. Maybe this really was Orion. My throat tightened with anxiety and anticipation. Being a human in an elite, secret club of lustful gods wasn't a game to be played lightly. If I disappeared, no one here would talk.

As the manor unfolded itself before my eyes, awe replaced any fear I felt. The ceilings climbed several stories up, but that wasn't the most impressive thing. The palace had similarly vaulted ceilings in its grand hall. This manor practically sparkled with magic. The flames in the man-sized fireplace burned green and pink. The drinks carried between immaculately dressed members of the club bubbled like potions in their delicate glasses. Large gray dogs with long limbs and sorrowful eyes sauntered between the legs of the guests. I spotted at least three.

And the members themselves—they were an assortment of striking, deathless males and females. Most were tall and human-shaped, as the majority of deathless beings were, but others had lion tails or miniature bodies. I couldn't help but stare at all the elegant, masked faces.

A large, warm hand pressed at the small of my back. An answering warmth pulsed between my legs at the touch.

"This is Willow," the stranger announced in his deep voice. He didn't speak loudly, but, judging by the way gazes slanted to give me appraising looks, everyone nearby heard him clearly. "She is interested in joining the club."

Willow wasn't my name, but I wasn't about to correct him. Everyone here probably had an alias. The wildness this club was famous for wasn't the kind of thing you wanted everyone to know. Right now, however, everyone at the Wildness Club looked so civilized in their outfits of forest green silk or cream embroidery. It was hard to believe I'd made it to the right place.

The stranger's hand slipped off my back. I wanted it there again. Everything about him was masculine and solid. Compared to most of the others, who were all beautiful in their own ways, he was rougher, thicker, but self-assured all the same.

I'd seen many deathless beings before, including leaders of the other Realms who came to visit my mother as a courtesy when they were in our lands. I'd met Basileus, god of the ocean, who ruled to the east. He had some of the untamed nature about him that I sensed in the stranger, but Basileus's skin was dark, punctuated with iridescent blue-green scales flush against his skin. I'd met Cytherea, the goddess of pleasure, who ruled the smallest of the Realms. She was tall and white and impossibly beautiful.

Kantharos was known for its culture. We had fewer wild woods and more manicured gardens. Safety in exchange for excitement.

Even our deathless acted like nobility in a way others didn't. At least when they were in public. I didn't think the Wildness Club counted as "public" but here they were, elegant and graceful and deadly, all sipping their drinks as if they were at a palace garden party. Despite how wondrous this manor was, here at the end of the civilized part of the queendom, I found myself getting annoyed. I didn't come here for polite small talk. I came here for...

When I couldn't verbalize it in my head, I gave a sour smile. If I couldn't even say it, could I do it?

"You want to... join?" asked a being who approached and towered over me. Its lips through the mask were scaly green, like the muzzle of a snake.

"Yes," I said, swallowing down any discomfort.

The being exhaled heavily, but it wasn't a sigh. It was more like the breath of a large animal. Was this a naga, the creature from terrifying bedtime stories? I'd thought those were all in the Far Realm with Hades...

"You look sssmall. Human."

"I am." There was no point in denying it. "But I still want to join."

The snake person observed me for a few seconds, sipped at the rim of the glass, and left.

Had I said something wrong? My eyes found the stranger working his way toward the enchanted fireplace. As if he sensed my gaze on him, he half-turned his head and met my look. He didn't offer to help introduce me to anyone else or return to my side. I was alone.

Fine. I'd gotten up the courage to come this far. I could meet these people and ask the questions burning in my chest.

Parties I could handle. Sidling up to a small group of deathless males, I said, "Excuse me, but do you know when the hunt is scheduled to begin?"

Eyebrows rose, glasses shifted in hands, and smirks spread over faces.

"What do you know of the hunt?" asked a man with unruly black hair who could almost pass as an exceptionally handsome Kantharan human. His voice was gravel-deep.

Curiosity and skepticism glowed in the attention everyone focused on me.

I swallowed on a dry mouth. A dog strode past my legs. "Orion hunts from midnight till dawn." It felt stupid telling the story like this, like a mother to a child. These mighty beings probably knew a thousand times more information about this than I did. "Whenever the fancy takes him. I've heard that, on nights when the Wildness Club meets, he goes alone, and doesn't hunt prey."

"Different kind of prey," put in a demi-god with shock-white hair. He licked his lips.

"Yes." My voice had grown hoarse. Trying to wet my mouth had no effect. "It's one of his favorite games at the club."

"Game," echoed the black-haired male. I couldn't tell if he was mocking me, correcting me, or something else. The masks made interactions harder, since I only got flashes of lips or eyes.

"How does he choose his prey?" I asked.

"Are you offering?"

Now was the moment. My heart pummeled my ribs. This fantasy, which had haunted my dreams for a year, could possibly come true tonight. It was the secret I held so close that not even my closest friends knew I craved it.

"Yes."

Their grins were positively wicked. I felt like prey already.

One laughed. "I underestimated this nasty girl. Can she follow through, do you think?"

"Those legs don't look ready for running," answered another.

"Bring her sparkling wine!" boomed the black-haired one.

I felt short of breath. I'd done it. I'd offered myself for Orion's hunt. The rumors were only vague in their language, since everyone liked euphemisms around here. The meaning behind all those village whispers was crystal clear. Orion liked to hunt down sex partners in the woods and fuck them till dawn.

A full glass was pressed into my hand. The liquid inside looked pink, gold, and green in different lights. I held it out. The deathless males did the same, clinking together our glasses. I chugged it all down in one long gulp. I half-expected the wine to be drugged. (Humans said such terrible things about the deathless in this club.) But it tasted crisp and fresh and unpoisoned. I wanted bottles of it for the palace.

"Orion's not the only one," said the male with white hair.

I suddenly wondered what this civilized party would turn into throughout the night. The idea made me want to return and see. Crazy, considering I hadn't even experienced one wild night yet.

"Do you hunt too?" I passed my empty glass off to a servant. Would I want to be hunted by one of the males standing here? Maybe. But my thoughts kept wandering to the stranger I'd met outside the door.

"Several do," he answered. His eyes raked down my body. "Or there are other ways to join."

"Like what?" I missed my wine glass already, since it gave me something to do with my hands. Regular parties didn't fluster me like this.

Thank goodness this wasn't a regular party.

I was done with those. I needed not only a break from all those inane pleasantries, but something so different I could never tell a soul. I wanted to be bad, to do something delicious and dangerous.

Someone nudged the white-haired male. He sighed resent-fully and said, "Don't ask me questions you don't want the answers to."

I did want the answers, but I also wasn't technically a

member of the club. This was some kind of introductory meeting or something. A test.

"All right, then. Does the hunt start soon?"

"You said yourself it begins at midnight."

There was no way to judge time in this place. I pressed my lips together and raised an eyebrow at him.

He chuckled. "You are very eager to be devoured, aren't you?" His eyes gleamed with hunger through the mask.

All the stories I'd heard of humans getting tricked by deathless plots rose to my mind. Gods and demi-gods from places other than Kantharos warring and scheming and enacting revenge. Actually eating people. Trapping and attacking them.

I'd walked right into this manor willingly, asking to be hunted. Sticky regret threatened to coat my insides.

But no one said Orion killed anybody. The rumors were salacious. No human sacrifices or nonsense like that.

I pulled in a breath. "I'm ready for Orion to chase me."

"Oooh!" the white-haired male crowed. "You think you stand a chance?"

"I think I want to be in the Wildness Club." I hurtled on, not stopping to check my words. "And I hear Orion is a ferocious lover who takes what he wants. I'm tired of being tame. I want him to take me."

The black-haired male gestured toward the fire. "Orion, you have an offer."

Warmth and excitement spread over my cheeks when they confirmed the man I'd met was the owner of the house, the club, and the hunt himself—Orion. He strode forward with slow confidence. The others in the circle were handsome, but he was more so, taut muscles straining under the surface of his finely tailored suit. What I could see of his face was ageless, older but in that way that grew in strength rather than diminishing it.

"An offer," he repeated, his eyes falling on me.

"Willow wants the hunt."

"I do," I confirmed, surer every second. If this man was the hunter, I'd gladly be the hunted.

"It's almost midnight," the white-haired male goaded.

Orion was unmoved. Instead, he stood looking at me, still and solid as a house beam. I couldn't tell what he was thinking —that I was too human, too small, too young, too inexperienced...? I felt too *something* with him looking at me like that.

"A word," he said.

The others dispersed as quickly as if they'd been ordered. If I needed any more proof that Orion was the master here, that was it.

The two of us stood in the center of the floor, but we were effectively alone.

"You want the hunt?"

"If... Yes."

"If what?"

I'd been about to say "if you're the hunter" but I couldn't make myself do it. So I pivoted. "If I'm guaranteed to live."

"You are." He said it simply, so sure of himself that it warmed me head to toe. I believed him. "But if you do this, you're mine for the night. Do you understand?"

I shivered, goosebumps pebbling over my exposed skin. "Yes."

"I don't think you do. *Mine*. There's no backing out."

I nodded.

"It's called the Wildness Club for good reason."

I nodded again.

"I'm not a gentleman."

He looked the part, but I could tell something simmered underneath, a wildness begging to come out. I concentrated on the muscular neck I could see between suit and mask.

"If you leave, we won't follow you," he said. "If you stay, unspeakable things will happen to you in the woods." He didn't say it as a threat, but as fact. Orion was king of this land even more than my grandmother was queen of it.

"I want the hunt," I said clearly.

He didn't smile, but lines rayed from his eyes.

My feet hurt, but excitement replaced the pain with something that felt good. I'd run barefoot if I had to. He promised unspeakable things.

"Very well. Ring the bell."

For a second, I was confused. What bell? But then one of the other guests scurried off to obey him.

The sound that followed wasn't the typical clang of a bell that you'd hear in bell towers in and near the palace. It was louder, more like a musical warning. Its message was clear: Stay out of the woods.

Except me. I'd be running through them in the dark.

Orion ushered me past the fireplace toward the back of the manor. Now that he had confirmed my participation, everything moved fast. Deathless men and women moved out of his way. More and more trailed us like water in his wake.

"You have half an hour," he said gruffly. His poised elegance was melting away into something else. He stripped off his suit jacket and handed it backward. Someone took it from him.

Without the jacket, he stunned me even more. That broad chest, those shoulders, that solid waist...

"Mask on or off, it's up to you. Doesn't matter to me," he continued. "Same with clothes."

Same with clothes? He didn't care if I ran around naked or not? I couldn't respond through my nerves and surprise.

"Don't leave the woods."

I felt like I was stuck on a galloping horse with no way to get off. This was happening now. I'd agreed to be his until sunrise. Agreed to anything he might want to do to me, short of murder.

Oh gods...

I ached with anticipation and fear.

After a moment of stillness with the club looking on, Orion waved his meaty hand impatiently. "Go!"

I ran. The back door looked out into untamed wilderness. Luckily, the moon was nearly full and the sky had no clouds. Even with that extra light, I could barely see. Moving as fast as I could without falling, which felt as slow as a dream, I traveled deeper into the forest. How far could I get in half an hour? I had a feeling it wouldn't matter. Orion would track me or smell me or whatever he did and I'd be in his clutches.

Half an hour was unbearable. It was enough time for me to second-guess everything I did, the choice to come here, the deep desire I had to be chased down and taken. It was also long enough for me to fantasize and get so wet I was angry he wasn't here to fuck me.

I kicked off my shoes. Why had I kept them on so long? My tender feet answered the question. Soil and roots and fallen twigs poked my soles. Little rocks were everywhere. I hoped they were rocks.

The ground sloped up. I had to scramble over bushes to reach the top of the swell. When I did, the trees opened up to a little meadow. It was easier to see there, since fewer trees blocked the moonlight. I hurried to the opposite end of the meadow and found a spot where I could hunker down behind a trunk and the large rock beside it, like a twisted game of hide and seek. From that spot, I might be able to see Orion approach. Orion, the hunter god, now hunting me.

My belly snaked into knots.

Half an hour was too long.

The forest smelled cool and leafy, lulling me toward calm after a few deep breaths. Birds and small rustlings quieted until all I could hear was myself. The air moving in and out of my nose, my pulse in my ear, the leaves underfoot when I shifted my weight.

Eyes glinted across the meadow. Confusion jolted through me. Those eyes were too low, too reflective-red, to be Orion's.

With a thick snuffling noise, a shaggy bear turned along the circumference of the clearing. I could see the outline of its body as it lumbered on quiet feet toward my hiding place. The eyes belonged to the bear.

Oh shit.

Was I being hunted by more than Orion? I knew with the instinctiveness of prey that the bear had scented me, and his turn toward my position wasn't coincidence. It was coming for me.

Why didn't I bring better shoes? The fancy shoes I'd worn to the party dangled from my hand. They wouldn't help. Running barefoot would hurt too, but at least I was less likely to turn an ankle.

The sound of the bear's breath mingled with my own. It was getting close.

I bit down on my lips to keep from making a sound. Orion had promised I wouldn't get killed out here. But where was he now? Blood raced through my veins, every heartbeat screaming *stay, run, stay, run, stay, run...*

My hands shook. Run. I would run.

With a burst of speed, I took off through the trees. Could bears zigzag? I had no idea, but that was my only plan. I'd bolt as fast as I could and try to find places where the trees grew together so the bear couldn't fit through. Wind whipped at my face, catching my hair.

Heavy, galloping steps matched my own.

Miraculously, I sped up, every ounce of energy channeled into getting away at whatever cost. That thing was huge. I couldn't let it catch me or...

Panting, feet shrieking, I flew through the woods. *Get away. Find somewhere it can't get you.* I could hardly see. Trees were black stains on a black background. What if I hit one and passed out? I'd be a bear's dinner.

A bellow erupted from the creature chasing me. My blood turned to ice. The gravelly breathing of the massive beast churned so close behind me I felt a huff of warm air hit the bare skin on my back. I bit back a sob.

A paw knocked me to the ground. I screamed as I tumbled, losing my shoes. I landed face upward.

The paw had a strange give to it, as if it were morphing or shrinking. No claws pierced my skin, but large hands kept grappling at my body, tearing at the clothes. The wet forge of a bear's breath emitted from a different body. A different being.

Orion.

Still transforming back into human shape, overlarge but with human features and naked male musculature, he ripped away my dress. The broad shoulders and square jaw I'd noticed at the party were exaggerated now. All his polite veneer shredded away to reveal the beast beneath.

Fear, relief, and racing adrenaline converted into a need so powerful I yelled something incoherent. My pussy throbbed, sopping wet.

Thank the Divine, because Orion had caught me and would take what he wanted. No foreplay. No warning.

With a desperate thrust, he shoved himself inside me. I tensed and writhed, but he fucked me with the intensity of rage. Sticks speared my back as I rubbed against the ground. Torn fabric surrounded me. His bear noises persisted and I shouldn't have liked it but my fantasy was here and nothing made me want to stop. I wanted his animal growls. I needed the sharp stab of his rigid cock. I was crying with pain and ecstasy. I didn't know myself.

And that was exactly what I wanted.

Orion was a wild creature above me. His frantic fucking slowed to measured, hard pumps and a jagged sigh as he spilled a thick stream of cum inside.

My heartbeat mirrored a jackrabbit's—so fast I thought I might pass out. He caught me and came, but I was still his for the night. For the first time since the party, he met my eyes.

For a long time, I'd imagined what he might do, but my ideas were more like dark fairy tales than the reality. This was far more frightening and wild. I felt out of control. Which was true. I'd just been fucked by a god half-transformed from a bear.

Orion's heavy breathing slowed, but his eyes didn't grow any less feral. If anything, they became more cunning. He was considering what to do with me.

I didn't say anything. Moment by moment, he returned to the masculine force I'd met at the party. Recognizable, at least. If anything, he was even more handsome than I'd thought him in his suit.

Here, in the forest under the bright moon, he gave into a part of his nature that I felt in mine too. He longed to hunt, and I longed to be hunted.

He snuffed out a breath. Under his gaze, I sat up, already achy from the force with which he took me.

"You didn't run very far."

It wasn't what I expected him to say. I couldn't tell if it was a criticism.

Raw from our wild coupling and my forbidden desires out for him to see, I felt stung. "I ran far enough."

His lips curled back in a toothy, wicked smile. A concession. He drew closer. "I would have smelled you anywhere." With a long inhale, he took in my scent.

After my long walk to the manor and the run through the forest, I doubted my scent was very nice, but Orion obviously disagreed. His eyes were practically black when he opened them again.

"After you agreed to my terms, nowhere was far enough," he rumbled. His hair looked thicker than it had at the party, wilder. Like a bear. He was bigger than before too. He had to be. His form dwarfed mine even more than he had when we'd stood next to each other, drinks in hand. He was thick and masculine in a primal way that made me want to give into him again. I was almost sorry the game was over.

He must have seen the disappointment in my face, because he added, "Oh no, I'm not done with you yet." He cupped my chin, and his expression was all hunter. The blazing intensity of his eyes glinted in the moonlight. I couldn't move. Even his cool fingers were calloused and strong.

My pulse chugged too fast.

"You're mine, you said." His hands slid down over the curves of my body. "Tonight, you're all mine."

"Tonight," I echoed. As much as I loved the danger, it *was* dangerous to be with this man, this god. I was his for the night and not beyond.

Unless I came back.

Then my sides compressed and the ground fell away. I chirped with alarm. But then I understood what had happened —Orion had picked me up. He threw me over his shoulder and ran. Ran like some beast through the woods, naked and savage and unstoppable. If wolves or bestial demi-gods lived in this forest, they'd retreat when they saw Orion coming. He was the wildest creature here.

Orion's touch was rock-firm but gentle enough not to bruise. Cool air flowed over my bare back.

I'd liked that dress. Now what would I wear to return to the palace?

The thought fled as Orion held me tighter, huffing with anticipation in my ear. Where were we going?

The terrain was rough. Even Orion's sure footsteps jostled as he headed toward his destination. Whatever that was. Away from civilization, I knew.

I scented the pool before I saw it. The freshness of water gently lapping. I frowned, but my immediate thought of protesting died away. It didn't matter that the water would be cold. Orion had obviously made up his mind.

He hurled me off his shoulder into the pond. Water splashed into my face, freezing my body. I went under. The water was deeper than I expected, so I emerged spluttering.

A second crash covered me with more cold. Hair stuck to my forehead and neck, all my carefully crafted beauty torn away. The expensive lace mask knotted in my hair, but it somehow stayed on, askew.

Arms yanked me forward against a hard body. I kicked to stay afloat. Wiping pond water out of my eyes through the slits in the stiff lace, I could finally see Orion observing me with feral anticipation. Even his smile was more a baring of teeth.

"I wanted you wet," he muttered, smoothing a hand over my scraggly locks. "Dripping."

"It's cold," I pointed out. Yes, he looked sexy like that. Gods, of course he did. But it was hard to do what he wanted in his cold, wasn't it?

His canines showed as his smile grew. "I know my forest, Willow."

"But you don't..."

"Know you?"

I had been about to say that.

But then his big hand caressed my side, my hip, and turned inward. Thick, calloused fingers found my clit and rubbed.

I squeaked and arched. The longer he went, the warmer I felt. Only the skim of surface tension still felt cool.

"You don't want me to know you." He leaned forward and took the lace in his teeth before letting the mask snap back. His fingers got more insistent as if they made his point too.

I wasn't kicking my legs anymore. Only Orion held me up. Between heartbeats, I wondered if he'd hurt me here, push me under.

But then that ache, that rubbing ache...

My head fell back.

"No." The command was short, sharp. He stopped what he was doing.

I pulled my heavy head upright, just as he swam suddenly the few strokes to shore, taking me with him. There was a shallow area only large enough to balance on before the mud fell away to deeper water. He stopped us there.

Lifting me out of the water would have been difficult for anyone, so I started crawling to the bank. A hand snatched me back. My feet stuck over the deeper part of the pond, but the rest of me sat in the shallower water. It didn't even lap up to my waist when I sat up.

Orion pulled himself out of the water. It streamed in moonlit streaks down his body. Maybe it was my awestruck focus on him, but he seemed bigger than he had at the party, as if the part that had shifted still moved beneath his skin.

With a bear-like snuff and a swish of his hips, he was on top of me again. Every move he made—we made—magnified in the quiet night because of the splashing, sucking shallow water. He held me down as he speared me again with his stone-hard cock.

Something about being wet in every way made me slicker than ever. It was like Orion knew. He pumped in and out, working me into a whimpering frenzy. I had nothing to hold onto but his arms, thick with muscle. He rode me hard and loud, splashing, announcing his dominance.

When I came, it was loud too—wet and inelegant. My legs trembled underneath him. He drove deep, deep, and pumped me full.

I lay half in and half out of the water, too tired to run. The pond felt good on my injured feet. We had nothing but our bodies left, plus my mask. How much more could we do? There were surely hours left until dawn. My belly clenched with new nerves, picturing my return as someone wrung out and hurting.

"Come," said Orion, hauling himself to standing. Just to gaze at him was a treat. Every angle offered a new delight.

When he offered his hand, I took it. Since when did the deathless offer to help a human? I was surprised he noticed how exhausted I already felt. Or maybe he just needed me to walk so he didn't have to carry me to our next location to fuck.

"A rest," he declared. From here, the pond looked pretty

under the stars. The ride there had been so hectic that I hadn't noticed. The spot he chose to stop might have made a good place for a bench if we'd been in the capitol.

I turned to evaluate him. "It isn't dawn." Without arousal to warm me up, the breeze was beginning to chill my wet skin.

"Plenty of time to make a meal of you." One side of his mouth lifted. "I'll fuck you again, don't worry."

Heat climbed to my cheeks. After what we'd already done, I was surprised I had any shame left.

No, not shame. Excitement.

"Good."

He laughed, a rich and heavy sound against the rhythmic shallow waves. "If you are still here when I wake, you will be a member of the Wildness Club."

I swallowed. A member of the club. That meant I could return and he could—

A gasp cut off my thoughts.

Orion was changing. His shoulders hunched and back bowed. His large face grew and elongated. Shaggy hair sprouted from his skin in ripples. Hands became paws tipped with fearsome claws.

The bear.

I froze, every instinct telling me to go, to run, to do something to preserve my life. This bear was several times the size of me. If it chose to attack, I wouldn't survive. If Orion wanted to chase me down again and savagely hump me, I couldn't protest or complain. My feet hurt. I couldn't go far.

The bear called Orion lay down, tucking his paws. I eyed him. He said I had to be here when he woke up, whenever that would be.

A smirk crossed my lips. The bear gave an answering look in its dark eye.

Approaching carefully, heart thumping, I extended a hand toward the creature. Orion didn't flinch or roar or do anything remotely frightening. I let my fingers sink into the deep, course fur and stroked his shoulder. The bear's eyelids lowered.

Slowly, I lay on the soft ground beside him, tucking myself against his warm fur. It would not be a problem to be here when he awoke. This promised to be the most comfortable sleep I'd had in weeks.

I felt as wild as the bear. Reaching behind me, I wrestled the ribbons from my tangled hair and took off the lace mask. Folding it, I set it beside me. The breeze caressed my face. When Orion awoke for another breathless, desperate fuck, he'd see the real me. Giving him that power felt even more reckless than offering myself for the hunt in the first place, but it was exhilarating too. No more masks. He was the hunter and I was the heir. The bear and the princess.

I snuggled against him. When I did, he let out a contented breath.

❦ 6 ❦

WARM WAX

Jacin treats Icarus to a special experience before they have to return to work.

Inspired by Icarus and Jacin's story in *Candle Wax and Sunlight*, this story includes explicit MM sex, strong language, wax play, ass play, romantic couple

"We only have an hour," I chuckled as Jacin pushed me back. "Do you think that'll be enough time for you?"

He leveled a look at me, but he never managed to look menacing. An amused smirk lived in his lips now.

After a hot morning of work at the smithy and the summer air breezing through our bedroom window, my shirt stuck to my back. I wasn't exactly fresh as a rose. Jacin, on the other hand, seemed fresh all the time. He smelled fantastic and was more comfortable in his own skin than he was wearing clothes. I thanked the gods for that regularly. If there was one reason the Sun God had chosen Jacin to be his consort years ago, it was his flawless body—hard where it needed to be hard, soft where it needed to be soft. I never got tired of looking at it.

The back of my knees hit the mattress. "You want me to lie down?"

He held a lit candle in one hand, so his manhandling of me was adorably uneven. "Yes. Legs off the side, please."

Just like I'd positioned him the first time we'd done this.

Stifling a smile, I obeyed, stretching myself out on the bed. The blankets near my head were still warm from Jacin's body heat. He'd been reading there, waiting for me to return. He wanted to try wax play right away, but I toyed with him before he could grab the candle. My mouth still tasted salty.

"Yes, just like that," he said.

I folded my hands over my middle. Jacin, already taller than me, loomed from the side of the bed. It was a good view. He wore only drawstring pants so the ridged expanse of his golden skin stretched up with no interruption. He gazed at me, eyes deep set. Contentment softened his features.

I knew what that look meant. I loved him too. My favorite was when I'd catch him looking while I did something normal, like fitting a mechanical brace or cooking dinner. I knew why people would look at Jacin like that, with a warm sense of wonder. He was beautiful and kind—everything I wanted to be and everything I always wanted near me. But that he would look at me like that... It set my heart beating faster every time.

"Shirt off, please."

Always so polite. The Sun King never appreciated that about Jacin. Hopefully burning part of the king's palace made life terrible for him. I liked to think he suffered for the way he treated Jacin.

I sat up and pulled my shirt over my head, only breaking eye contact when the fabric covered my vision.

Jacin's gaze roamed over my broad chest. Again, sweaty and kind of hairy. I shouldn't have been the object of this man's affection, but we were four years on, and he still gave me appreciative looks that warmed my blood.

"Do you want these off too?" I teased, hooking my thumb in my waistband. Jacin had asked the same thing the first time I'd suggested wax, back when we were forbidden to touch.

"Of course, yeah." He smiled. The candle dripped down the pillar.

I watched it, anticipation building in my gut as I stripped down and lay back on the blankets. Hard morning sunlight streaked the bed. I adjusted so it wasn't in my eyes.

Between sucking Jacin off a few minutes ago and now preparing for a new erotic experience, I was long and painfully stiff. If he'd set the candle down and simply given me a hand job—he disliked giving blow jobs, and that was fine—I would have been very happy. Well, I would have tensed and moaned and begged, more likely.

"Oh, Icarus," he sighed. "Ready?"

I ached even more at the adoration in his voice. Struggling to keep still, I smiled up at him. "Whenever you are."

He tucked a golden-brown curl over one ear and surveyed my body as if looking for the perfect place to start. Finally, he dipped a finger in the wax to test the temperature. Satisfied, he raised the candlestick over the lower half of my body.

I flexed, preparing. I didn't expect him to start there.

"Pretend this wax is me touching you," he whispered, and poured.

Hot wax hit the top of my thigh. I sucked in a breath. Gods, but I got harder somehow. Would I even make it through his whole display?

"Good?" he asked.

I nodded, my hands forming fists.

He trailed the wax up my thigh to my hip, the divot where it led to my cock.

"Shit," I gritted out, slamming my eyes closed.

He lingered there awhile, letting the wax slide slowly down toward the root of my shaft. I started shaking.

Finally, he pulled up. I panted and opened my eyes again. The candle needed to burn down further to get more liquid wax to pour. Jacin gave me a wicked look.

For someone so sweet and thoughtful, he knew how to take control when he wanted to. For that and so many other reasons, I was usually the bottom. Jacin had no control over his own life for more than twenty years. When he finally chose something for himself, it was his relationship with me. Had anyone ever been so lucky? So yes, I loved when he fucked me senseless.

Right now, though, if he didn't hurry up, I was going to spring from this bed and bury myself inside him until we both came.

I throbbed with need. "Keep going," I demanded, wanting it to come out flirtatious, but sounding more desperate than anything.

Jacin bit his lip. Shit. He'd had that tic since before we met, but every time he did it, I wanted to devour him.

"Be patient."

"I don't want to be patient." My heartbeat charged forward. "I want you to get on with it."

"The wax needs time." His eyes fell on my erection.

"Don't know that I have time," I said with a dark, pained chuckle.

"Okay, okay." He returned his attention to the candle. Looked burned down enough to me. "Here we go."

Slowly, he tipped the candle over again, this time above my chest. Sticky wax got trapped in my dark chest hair. Jacin swirled a design that ended with drops falling on my nipples.

"Jacin," I gasped.

He laughed. "Good?"

"Please..."

A line stream of wax drew a line down the center of my torso. Down, down...

I gathered blankets in my fists.

"Oh, we're out."

I craned my neck to face Jacin dead-on. "What?"

His cheek dimpled. "Patience."

I closed my eyes again. "I'm sorry I ever did this to you."

"I'm not. It felt delicious. Just wait a second."

His open manner flooded me with warmth for him again. Now if he would only finish getting me off. I could hardly bear to lie still with Jacin standing half-naked above me, and remnants of wax clinging to my nipples and the inside of my hip.

My breath shallowed as he bent forward again. The candle hovered right over my aching cock.

When the wax dropped, I groaned loudly. "Fuck!"

Jacin traced the head and traveled down the shaft to my balls.

"Oh gods. Fuck. Fuck!" My fists trembled.

A click meant he'd set the candlestick down.

Instead of wax, the next sensation was fingers, a palm, his whole hand massaging me. Expertly circling the head and pumping the shaft while cupping my balls, he made me lose my mind. I writhed against the mattress. I could hardly open my eyes to watch Jacin rubbing and slapping me as if he were in a trance. His lips parted as he worked. His glorious chest rose and fell in breathless excitement.

I couldn't stand it. Sitting up, I grabbed his face and kissed him. With our faces still smashed together, he worked me. I made ungodly noises into his mouth. Then he was moaning into mine.

I tensed, balls clenching. My groans turned into whimpers and then a guttural rhythmic cry as I came hard over both of us.

"Oh my gods," I said, delirious.

I felt Jacin smile against my mouth. He still hadn't let go.

"That was..."

"Good, right?" he said.

I flopped backward onto the bed, half out of sheer exhaustion and half so I could give him the look of derision he deserved. Yes, it was good. Obviously, it was good. Thick specks of cum covering his chest kind of good.

I lay there for a minute, returning to normal. Finally, I sighed. "Very good."

Jacin released my cock and lay down next to me, angling on his side. Sunlight backlit his head and shoulder. My gaze traced the bright golden line.

He kissed me on the cheek. "I've made you messy, though."

Jacin was cleaner than me, by personality and habit. His side of the room was cleaner. He used scented oils in his bath when he could. No one was here to tell him to keep things perfectly spotless and organized like there was at the palace, but he kept a similar mindset. On bad days, a scented bath and scrub could make him feel all right again.

I drew my hand down the wax crusting over my body. It felt soft, still pliable since it rested on my raging body heat. "I'll clean it up."

"Worth it, though."

"Worth it," I agreed, tipping my chin up.

Jacin met my lips. "You look good like this."

I smirked. "Do I?" I pretended to tuck my hands behind my head in an excuse to flex my arms. They were probably my favorite feature of mine, thickly developed enough that I often had to settle for oversized shirts to fit my arms and shoulders.

He eyed them hungrily. I knew that look too. It wasn't the adoring tender one that meant *I love you.* It was the look he got when he wanted another round. Gods, he had stamina.

I leaned my head back. I'd never say no, but I was tired and I'd just come hard. I needed a minute.

He knew it too. Instead of diving right in again, he kissed my bulging arms, my chest with wax on it, down to my belly button. That started to perk me up again.

"How much of our hour's left?" I asked.

His hair feathered over my skin with his next sweet kiss. "I bet it's enough."

"Don't you think that's dangerous, cutting it close like that?" I teased. "What if someone walked in?"

"To our bedroom?" He rose up to look at me, brow furrowed. Maybe he couldn't tell if I was joking.

The shop was attached to the house, but no one came in here. It was off-limits to everyone but us.

"Imagine, they come in to get their splint and massage and instead they hear..."

Jacin's eyes blazed. "What?"

My lips curled. We sometimes played this game, but usually in bed at night. I'd tell him all the ways I wanted to touch him, to pleasure him, to make him come apart. If I did my job right, he'd be whimpering and touching himself. We'd both hold off until one of us gave in. He said my words were almost better than hands, so I did what I could to bring him to the brink.

I lifted up on my elbow so we reclined face to face. Jacin's cock already pointed straight at me.

"They hear the slap of my groin against your ass as I drive into you."

Jacin's lips parted and eyes grew hooded.

"My moans as I insist how perfect you are. And you groan too because I'm deep inside you, thrusting fast."

His cheeks darkened.

"And I'm not finished. I kiss your shoulder blade because it's so damn perfect."

Fuck, I was getting myself worked up with this fantasy.

After a few rapid heartbeats, Jacin said, "Then what?"

"You want more?"

He nodded.

"The bed is squeaking and you are cursing—because you do that now." Jacin wasn't one to swear every day, but my blow job earlier had made him yell out the work *fuck!* loud enough for people walking by outside to hear.

"I slip my fingers in your mouth to suck on," I continued.

With the speed of compulsion, he gripped my hand and fed two fingers between his lips. My vision went hazy as his tongue slid and pulsed around them.

"And I..." My mind stopped functioning. I'd meant so say something filthy about grabbing his shaft as it bobbed underneath us. But words were necessary. Words were gone.

Jacin scanned my too-hot body. After sucking a few more seconds in the most sensual way I could imagine, he popped my fingers out of his mouth, dripping with his spit. "Do it."

I rarely fucked him. It was important to both of us that

Jacin feel in control, especially when we had sex. "Sure?" I breathed. I was on fire.

Then Jacin straddled me on hands and knees.

Thoughts. Gone.

He kissed me, and then—*fuck me!*—rolled his body against mine. Nothing was sexier than Jacin on an average day. Today, he decided to be all my fantasies in one.

When I stirred, mouth dry, he released me from the cage he'd created so I could roll off the bed. My legs felt unsteady, but I moved them to the foot of the bed. While I did, he whipped off his drawstring pants. Jacin was so gorgeous there —those strong legs and perfectly shaped ass. I could hardly breathe.

"Oil," I croaked. I had no spit, and that wasn't great lubricant anyway.

Jacin moved in a way I would dream about, stretching forward, hips still in the air, to open an end table drawer and draw out the vial of oil. Arching back into position, he handed it to me. There was a chance he knew how erotic that move was, but Jacin never fully understood how much he affected me. He was my landscape, my home, the most beautiful person I'd ever known, inside and out.

I poured a palmful of oil into my hand and went to spread it on my cock first. There was still excess wax. An insane giggle gusted from my lips as I hurriedly rubbed it off. I was so sensitive already. My short thumbnail peeling off flakes of half-dried wax didn't help.

Fighting for breath, I finished scraping it off and ran the oil up my shaft. The rest of the oil was for Jacin. My fingers still buzzed, slightly wet, from being inside his mouth. The combination of my intense arousal and the opportunity to palm his ass was almost too much. I took the chance greedily, kneading him, even giving him a soft smack on the behind.

At my first touch, Jacin sank down with his arm over his eyes. Always so responsive. My stomach roiled with eagerness.

Since I didn't do this often, I had to prime him. All the oil I'd poured out smeared over the two of us. It coated my hands.

"Okay," I huffed, unable to form a more cohesive sentence.

Jacin apparently knew what I meant, because he nodded into the crook of his arm.

I shoved my middle finger slowly into him. He was so tight, squeezing around me.

A high-pitched moan escaped him.

"Okay?"

He nodded again. "Keep going." The words smothered against his arm.

I did. My first knuckle passed the ring of muscle, then the second. Jacin's bare back convulsed. I eased out, then back in. It was easier the second time. I leaned forward to get my finger all the way in. In, out. Repeating until the wet, rhythmic sound filled the room.

"Oh," he gasped. "Icar—" He turned his head. From here I could see his grimace.

I picked up the pace, plunging as deep as my finger could go. My cock was nearly twice as long as my finger at the moment, with this fodder filling it with expectation.

"Yeah?" I said.

Jacin made a helpless sound in answer.

"Yeah?" I gripped him harder with my free hand. Heart pounding, I pulled my finger out and squared myself in position behind him.

I was long and stiff and the head was big and I honestly didn't know if I'd fit in today. But I was damn well going to try.

Setting myself against his entrance, I rubbed my slick cock up and down. Jacin's mouth opened with new ecstasy. I was almost sorry to make him tense up again with some pain. Almost.

I fed the tip inside, a nearly impossible fit.

As I expected, all his muscles flexed compulsively—that glorious back, those arms, and even his ass.

"Try to relax," I managed. I felt frenzied, but Jacin mattered most, always.

After a few breaths, his shoulders lowered. I pushed a little further inside, rocking back and forth in small strokes. He gripped me tight enough to be a fist. Sweat rolled down my neck. Deeper, deeper.

"Ah, yes!" he said against the blankets.

I moved a little faster, enough to thrust at the end each time. Air gusted from my lungs. I found myself leaning over him as I went deeper, wanting his ass, his back, his hair against me. By the time I made it all the way in, I hugged his chest, holding him fully against my body. His noises sounded different this close, and I craved each forceful breath and impassioned shout.

Mostly it was mumbling, begging. "Oh, Icarus, gods. Yes! I just... I can't... Oh fuck! More. Oh, you feel..." It made me wild.

I probably sounded the same. "I want to... fuck you harder."

"Oh my gods, do it!"

With one arm barred diagonally across his chest and the other straight across his abdomen, I lifted him flush against me. His hair got in my eyes and in my mouth. But now I stood up and had more room—maybe imaginary, but it seemed like it—to drive into him with all the force I wanted.

Jacin sat up on his knees on the bed. If the weather and the work and the sex hadn't heated my blood before, the sight of him rolling his head back on my shoulder to let me hammer into him still would have made my skin feel tight with heat. I'd explode, probably. The perfect way to go.

With a growl, I backed up and smacked into him hard enough to make a muted crack when our bodies collided. I did it again. And now jackrabbit fast. My hips moved quick enough to be a workout. I couldn't get enough of him. Couldn't get enough of the way he arched or grabbed hold of me everywhere his hands could reach.

"Ah yes, fuck yes!" I grunted.

No matter how he writhed, he wouldn't escape my hold. His groans got louder.

"Oh fuck!" I yelled, and lowered my hand on his belly to bump his raging hard on. I'd make him come with me.

He was squirming, in a fever. When I caught his dick, his hand met mine and helped stroke it just the way he liked. He knocked me off to pump himself and I butted in to finish the job. It was everything.

I couldn't hold on.

Scooping my hips up into him again, white burst in my vision and my balls emptied. He cried out loudly as he came right after.

I slumped over him. For a few heated seconds, I crushed him under me on the bed as I lay on top of him. With a sigh, I rolled off. I was disgusting, a mass of sweat and cum and wax. I was even drooling. Very attractive.

But damn, that was good.

"Fuck, Jacin," I breathed.

He curled his fingers through my chest hair. "That was amazing." He looked flushed and beautiful, as usual.

If anyone walked in and saw the two of us, no one would understand why he was with me.

If anyone walked in.

I threaded my hand through his. "It's been an hour, hasn't it?" I shut my eyes, preparing for the answer.

"Oh!" He bolted upright, scanning for his clothes.

I cursed and chuckled. We were late.

Normally, we valued being punctual for our clients, who usually had some ailment or need. I made slings and artificial limbs; Jacin massaged creams and ointments into joints and muscles. We were responsible.

Not today. But it wasn't every day that Jacin erotically poured warm wax over me or let me fuck him until I was barely coherent. I regretted nothing. In fact, I wanted Jacin to lie back down so I could scoop him in my arms.

"All the wax is still on you," he said, pulling on his pants.

"Mm."

"We have a client," he laughed, diving at me and pulling off the larger pieces still intact against my leg and chest.

I pulled him in for a kiss. He surrendered to it for a moment—a version of that soft look he gave me sometimes when I wasn't looking. His mouth enjoyed mine, melting against me.

He pushed himself back upright. "This blanket is ruined."

"Washable," I corrected, finally standing and handing him the corner.

He used it to rub off the drying cum.

"I like when you're a mess for me," I confessed.

With a smirk, he handed the blanket back for me to wipe off. Unfortunately, he found a loose-fitting shirt and slung it on.

"I like being a mess for you."

My belly somersaulted. "I love you. And"—I joined his search for clothes—"I wish we could be a mess together without somebody interrupting."

"They're a paying customer. And you know how we help—"

"Yes, yes." I found a fresh set of clothes and put it on. Dressed, I cheated another look at Jacin. Even disheveled, he practically glowed. I'd spent nights not sleeping because *that* was sleeping next to me. How could I stop gazing at that face?

"We need to go," he said.

"Yes, I know."

"Your hair looks crazy."

"I figured." I ran a hand through it. Jacin tried the same thing, but my unruly curls rarely obeyed. After this kind of morning, those curls would never behave.

His hand paused against my head. One of those looks lit up his face.

"I love you," he said.

The Sun God could go fuck himself if he couldn't appreciate this human.

"I bet I love you more. Also," I added as we headed toward the door, "I hope you'll let me do that again, because I'm pretty sure I ascended to demi-god status at least."

Jacin laughed, hushing me as we opened the door to meet our waiting client.

IF YOU LIKED THIS STORY, CHECK OUT *CANDLE WAX AND Sunlight* or any of the other Deathless Love books in the series.

They're interconnected standalones, so you can begin wherever your mood or curiosity takes you!

AYAME'S PLEASURE

Ayame, a minor goddess from Menos, has had a shitty week. It's time to find the ultimate way to unwind with the help of five eager partners.

This original story includes explicit sex, strong language, sex work, orgy, whips, choking, anonymity, MMMMMF, and voyeurism

My jaw jutted as I adjusted the thin straps of my wine-colored dress. I hadn't worn this gown in a long while. Its neckline plunged almost to my navel and the flowy material floated just long enough to cover my ass. If I danced at this party, the others would get a good view.

Let them.

Besides, I hadn't decided if I'd dance at all. The tension building in my body over the past week needed a bigger release than grinding against some demi-god.

My eyes, when I caught my reflection in the window, gazed

with a clear message. *Fuck off.* I gave a dark chuckle. Smart people would stay away if I looked like that.

It had been a hell of a week. Storms destroyed the best part of my home, a rock and flower garden I'd spent decades perfecting. It was beautiful enough that people came to southern Menos just to see it.

When I was young, I'd learned my color-altering power by practicing on one particular crescent-shaped rock. Losing that hurt the most. After days of searching, I had to accept that the flood had swept it too far to find. And then my boyfriend—my fucking ex—refused to take my loss seriously. Laughed at me. *Laughed at me* for getting choked up about it. I told him I'd take the crescent-shaped rock over him. He said the nastiest things.

Even after a thorough search, I knew there were probably more of his things in my house. They lurked there like poisoned slime. I dreaded looking into a cabinet or trunk I rarely opened only to find something that belonged to him.

I asked a few of my deathless friends to attend the party with me. They all said no, even after I offered to pay the entry fee. So here I was, going alone.

Even better, I thought, gritting my teeth. Apart from the look of murder on my face, I looked damn sexy. Tall and dark, with lush hips and smooth skin. Long black hair fell to my mid-back.

Without company, I could do whatever the fuck I wanted.

Menos wasn't known for its parties, but one demi-god hosted regular events to rival the legendary Dio's. I'd gone a few times in the past. Vague memories of flowing wine and dim lights and a mass of dancers were all that remained. Oh, and there were private rooms. That was where I was headed tonight.

Leaving everything but my entry fee, I let the room dissolve around me. Darkness surrounded me as I walked through the air toward my destination. It squeezed tight before opening into a new space: the entrance to the party.

Laughter and music rose from inside the building, which was warded. No god or demi-god could appear directly inside without paying.

I shoved money at the door guard and stalked inside. Tonight, I'd lose myself. If I was lucky, I'd find myself. I'd... something. My muscles and skin felt tense. Even the scent of sparkling musk didn't calm me.

The interior was warmer than outside. Darker, too. My house burst with color, but here, the most interesting thing to see was the crowd of mostly deathless Nalian and Menos people moving to the live music. The atmosphere started to dig under my skin. Good. My tension and rage separated me from the carefree wildness, but I liked watching all those dark, beautiful bodies together. The sight made me clench my thighs together. The dress barely covered me.

Time to find those exclusive rooms.

Striding along the edge to the back of the large room, I passed the musicians—several drummers and woodwind players caught up in a frenzy of sound—and found two doorways.

"These are private," said the horned male outside. He was pale but too tall to be a faun. Deathless then. Good looking.

"I know. I'm good for it."

The not-faun looked skeptical.

I couldn't help the curl of my lip. "Ayame. Have you not heard of me?"

I wasn't exactly famous, but a long life in the same community with a household feature that used to be news, meant that most people around here knew who I was.

My name did appear to register, because the not-faun guard relaxed his stance. "Of course." He gestured to one door, then the other. "There are males through here, females through here."

I chose the door featuring males. Music muted as the door closed behind me. No one else had taken advantage of this exclusive option. I had arrived sort of early. The only people in here with me were five gorgeous males lounging in different positions and stages of undress on a platform in the middle of the room. One was eating a piece of bread and talking while another, totally nude, walked across the room.

One with warm brown skin a little lighter than mine approached. Behind him, the others perked up, taking in my appearance.

"Are you here for some company?" he asked. This leader was the only one fully dressed. He wore a tan outfit and a variety of golden ear cuffs and rings. His eyes were nearly black.

I smirked at his language. "Yes."

"Deathless, human, or other?"

"I'm deathless." Among some, it was impolite to ask whether someone was a full goddess or demi-goddess. I didn't really care. Being a minor goddess didn't carry a huge amount of prestige anyway.

The leader's full lips lifted. "Good."

Deathless females could control their cycles at will. Normally, that meant we could avoid getting accidentally pregnant, one of my favorite things about being deathless. Just imagine...

The four others approached with curious or eager expressions.

"I'm surprised you come here for entertainment, when you are..." The leader didn't finish his statement, but let his eyes rake over me.

I pressed my lips together. I wasn't interested in meeting someone new. I was interested in being fucked.

With an appreciative hum, the leader indicated the first male in line, the one who'd been walking across the room when I came in. He was light-skinned and dark haired, with lean, defined muscles and only a short pair of pants to obscure my view of his body. Thick brows lowered over intense, deep-set brown eyes. In one of them was a diagonal scar that got lost in his hair line.

"Mace," the leader said. "Don't worry about his real name. If you want someone who likes rough play, choose him. He'll punish you."

An approving dimple appeared in Mace's cheek and his arms flexed as if he were ready to be unleashed.

"The next is Anchor."

The largest man nodded his shaved head once to acknowledge the leader's introduction. I rose only to his bulging shoulder.

"He's usually requested because of his large... offering." The leader gave a suggestive smile.

My eyes fell to the brown pants Anchor wore. I saw exactly what they were talking about. Anchor. Fitting name.

"And here, he goes by Mouth."

"Mouse?"

The man in question corrected me by flicking his big tongue playfully.

Oh shit. Okay.

He gave me a wink.

"And Devotion." The leader pointed to the final man down the line, the one who was fully naked. Devotion had a light beard over a bronzed face, thick wavy hair, and well-built arms. Sultry lashes framed green eyes that met mine in an open invitation. "He's a romantic."

Facing these five already began to replace the stress from this shitty week, transforming it into anticipation.

"What's your pleasure?" asked the leader.

Mace, the one who liked it rough.

Anchor, the one with the biggest dick.

Mouth, the one with the oral fixation.

Devotion, the one who'd worship me.

"What about you?" I asked.

The leader seemed surprised by the question, but quickly returned to his smooth manner. "I enjoy control, direction. I'll watch any one of them."

I made up my mind immediately. "All five."

The leader raised his eyebrows. Mouth licked his lips.

"We're exclusive for a reason," the leader said, "but if you—"

"Here." I placed a blank piece of parchment with my seal on it, and the seal of Menos, into his hand. I was tired of being dismissed and underestimated. Tired of things going wrong. I didn't care how much it cost to reserve all five males for the night. I'd pay it. "Just write how much and I'll have it delivered tomorrow."

It was impractical to carry coins around, especially in a barely-there dress like this, so I brought owing papers.

"All five?" he confirmed. "At once or consecutively?"

"At once."

It made me glad to see that the men's eyes gleamed at the

prospect. They seemed excited. Good. One of the reasons I'd chosen this place—besides the lack of options—was that I'd heard that the working conditions were better here than elsewhere. These men kept their pay. They reserved the right to say no. They could quit if they wanted. All the things that should have been basic etiquette for any sex worker, but that weren't true for everybody.

These males liked sex and wanted to do this. If I hadn't heard it through rumors, I'd have read it in their eager body language.

The leader and I finished marking the parchment. "In here," he said.

At the far end of the room was another door. We all filed toward it.

This was mad. This was a lot. This was...

By the Divine, this was perfect.

The inner room drowned out any echo of the music outside. Lit by only one round lantern hanging from the ceiling, it held a bed large enough for us all in one corner, shelves of implements, soft couches, large cushions, chains, blankets, chairs, whips, scents, oils, and a water feature that made it seem like it was raining into a recess in the floor.

I didn't think I'd be overwhelmed, but I didn't know where to begin.

Devotion cupped my face. His sweet breath warmed my lips, but he didn't close the distance.

"You can stop us at any time," said the leader, settling into a chair by the door. "Simply ask."

"All right," I said, as Mouth stripped the sleeves of my dress down my arms from behind.

It would take a lot for me to say no. These males knew

what they were doing, and I was ready for them to do their worst.

Mouth's dark hands caressed my sides as he eased the dress all the way off. Mace took it from him and flung it aside.

"Wash first," the leader instructed.

Devotion released my face and fetched a towel by the falling water. My attention tore between him and the others, all undressing to match. They were a breathtaking group. I wanted to touch them all.

Although I'd partied, I'd never done something like this, so I wanted to see how they'd begin before I took too many liberties. Once I felt comfortable, though, I planned to run my nails through Devotion's hair, and wrap my legs around Anchor's thick bulk.

Mace stalked around the outside of our group, and Anchor sat in a padded chair opposite the leader, leaving Devotion and Mouth to rub a wet cloth over my body. Together, they lifted me to take off my shoes and wash my feet.

So they can suck anywhere they want to.

The thought made me dizzy in the best way. I was so glad no friends had come with me. I had all these men to myself. Their care made me feel more like the goddess I was.

With Mouth carrying my legs by the ankles, held slightly apart, and Devotion holding me under my arms, I felt weightless. They settled me on something firm. Something big. Something hard.

Anchor reached around to resettle me on his lap. It cost him no effort at all to pick me up.

Suddenly, fingers threaded through my hair, gripping hard and slowly pulling my head back. I looked up into Mace's scarred face. My pulse beat in my throat and throbbed between my legs. His smile was savage. "Ready?" he snarled.

Anticipation built to a peak. I opened my lips but no words fell out.

Say something, damn it.

"Give me everything you have."

He yanked my hair harder until my head was forced back against Anchor's shoulder, neck exposed. I couldn't see what was happening. But gods, *gods*, could I feel it.

Hands pressed my legs apart, exposing my dripping pussy. A tongue, large and talented and mobile, took a slow lap before lips suctioned over my clit and the real fun began. Precise flicks teased my sensitive spot until I writhed in Anchor's arms.

His hard-on bumped my lower back. I wriggled backward to rub against it. Anchor rolled his hips in small movements to meet me.

From above, Devotion bent to kiss my open mouth and run his hands up to cup my breasts. I met his kiss greedily. It made me wetter, which made Mouth growl between my legs, which made me squirm harder, which excited Anchor.

I moaned into Devotion's mouth.

The leader spoke from his chair. "Lift her up, Anchor. Fuck her. And Mace, bind her hands."

A cry broke from me as my arms were pulled backward and bound together at the wrist with leather straps. Mace tied them expertly. Going around Anchor's huge form made it painful, though.

Devotion stood back long enough for Anchor to haul me up and position me over his enormous cock. Mouth never reduced his suction or the way he made me his feast.

A sob of pain and sopping need ripped from my throat when Anchor lowered me on top of him. The head of his dick barely fit, but then there was more and he kept pushing in.

A sharp sting to my breast distracted me from the aching stretch.

My eyes flew open. Mace held a small black whip. He flicked his wrist, and the end cracked against my nipple. He watched me hungrily as I fought against the restraints. I couldn't soothe the pain or rub the needy places.

"Take that cock," said Mace, lowering the whip to close his hand around my throat. If I wheezed hard, I could catch a breath, but his fingers were tightening.

And Anchor's cock kept splitting me open and—*gods!*—he flexed in for his first thrust. I shuddered violently.

Mouth's broad tongue kept working, licking my wetness as if he couldn't get enough. It was sensual. Indecent. Half the time I felt his nose buried against me, heightening the sensation.

"Take it," Mace demanded again.

"Harder," said the leader. I didn't know who he was talking to.

The men seemed to understand, though, because Mace let go right as Anchor placed his big hands on my hips and started driving into me. I gasped, bouncing on Anchor's cock. The world went dark, then white.

"That's it," Devotion said encouragingly. He eased me back against Anchor's chest and flung his leg over to straddle me.

Mouth disengaged to make room.

Devotion's movement crushed me down on Anchor's huge length, but I stopped bobbing so much. With adoration in his eyes, Devotion took in my sweating form. His erection rested against my belly as he smoothed his thumb over my stinging nipples. Rocking from Anchor's thrusts, Devotion lowered himself down to suck my breasts gently, searchingly. His hands explored my skin. It was heavenly.

Eventually, the leader laughed, "Take turns, you greedy bastard."

With a lingering parting kiss on my lips, Devotion rose.

"I want her," Mace declared, undoing my bindings. He pulled me roughly off Anchor's lap. I felt immediately empty, slippery and open.

Mace slammed me against the wall, right by the leader's head, and plunged into me. I fought for breath, but he grabbed my hair again and pressed against me with all his weight.

"You like that?" he demanded, fucking me hard into the wall.

I made a desperate noise that was apparently enough for him. My foot left the floor and I thrashed. Dizziness made me overcompensate. Then the second foot rose too. Mace held me up with too-strong hands and his hard cock pumping into me.

What was happening?

Delirious, I looked over his shoulder. Mouth and Devotion held my bent legs.

Devotion, as his name suggested, was the first to kneel. The floor was stone. It must have hurt. But he slipped my toes into his mouth as if nothing else mattered. The warmth of his tongue on my toes made me lose my mind.

I cried out again.

"Yeah?" Mace said.

Mouth sucked on the other foot.

"Fuck!" I screamed.

Mace seemed to take that as an order. He rode me until my spine bruised against the hard wall. My muscles tensed as he rode the places I needed that friction and the others were sucking and...

"Fuck! Ah!" I shook hard as I came.

When I gathered my wits, Devotion was smoothing my hair, carrying me to the bed. Around his body, I could see Mace following, wiping his lips, chest heaving. At the bed already were Anchor and Mouth. And near my head was the leader. His clothes were still on, but he watched me with a glazed expression of lust that made me want him to join us too.

"We're going to try something," the leader said in a voice more measured than the look on his face.

Devotion set me down on the soft blankets.

"Anchor."

As if he knew exactly what to do, Anchor rocked the mattress by crawling over it to the center, where he lay face up. His erection hadn't receded. If anything, he'd swollen even bigger than before. I doubted I could wrap my hand around him with my fingers touching.

"Mouth."

He obeyed the leader's understood order by closing the distance between us and kissing me deeply. I found my own taste on his tongue. He was the best kisser so far. I melted into him. He coaxed me onto the bed, moving me with strokes of his fingers until we both straddled Anchor—me facing forward and Mouth facing back. He found my clit so easily I bucked at first before whimpering and thrusting against his hand.

Then, somehow, he had gripped Anchor's shaft and was feeding it into me. Again, I stretched wide, pulsing to make room for him. Mouth faded away, getting off the bed.

"Devotion."

The leader had a perfect grasp of how to position and command everyone. I wondered what he tasted like, what his preferences were.

The mattress depressed, and Devotion settled on his knees

behind me. I glanced back to catch him gazing at my round ass with a level of appreciation I only dreamed of.

When a hand pressed on my upper back, I whipped around. The leader pushed me down, flush against Anchor's wide chest. His touch was insistent, not cruel but experienced in the ways of pleasure. I wanted to learn everything.

"Devotion," he said again.

Devotion slicked something wet over his cock and pushed against my back entrance. His sigh sent shivers down my back.

"Now," said Anchor, who, up to that point, hadn't said a word. He frowned at Devotion, obviously eager to get going.

Setting hands on my hips, Devotion angled his hips so he could push in from behind. With Anchor filling me up, could I fit him too? I fidgeted to make more space.

"Oh," he breathed, going deeper.

Anchor grunted. He had to have been able to feel Devotion's dick pressing against his.

My skin felt hot and tight. These two gorgeous males filling me from both sides...

Slowly, they started moving. Slow at first, anyway. They soon got as carried away as I felt, jostling and grinding and smacking in deep.

Sweat rolled down my throat to my chest.

"Mace." The name came out hoarse.

Mace lost no time. He sprang up, cock stiff, onto the bed.

"Gonna be a good girl?" he murmured, gripping the back of my head.

"Yes."

Bending his knees so he could position his dick in front of my mouth, he held himself and said, "Open."

I did. His cock was heavy and warm and stone-hard. It tasted salt-savory.

He didn't go slow. He knifed forward, demanding.

Beneath me and behind me and in front of me, three males fucked me like they couldn't stop. Another orgasm built and I convulsed, choking on Mace's cock. Waves of pleasure shook me, aching, wetting Anchor's shaft.

He grew more desperate beneath me, taking me faster, letting out feral noises.

"Yes," I encouraged.

With a loud groan, he emptied himself inside me.

Devotion sounded like he was begging. His groin pressed against my ass each time he rolled his hips.

"Fill her up," the leader said.

"Ah! Ah..." Devotion sped up, taking instead of giving for the first time, and exploded into me.

I was limp and full of cum.

But not ready to stop.

"That's a good girl," said Mace. "Want more cum? Want more?" He pushed me off Anchor and down onto the blankets. His feral look of need as he took me again made me need him too.

"Yes," I answered.

"Yes?"

"Give it to me."

With a snarl, he pumped violently into me. His hands found my pert nipples and squeezed, merciless.

I screamed.

He kept going, mixing pain and pleasure.

Strangest of all, I got kissed upside-down by someone kneeling at my head. Mouth. I knew that tongue.

Mace's growls grew wilder, his thrusts sharper. Then in a burst of release, he came too, mixing his cum with Anchor's.

"That's good."

Panting, I looked at the leader, who watched us closely.

"Mouth," he said, eyes darting up from my face to his. "I want a turn."

My insides flipflopped. I shouldn't have had room to feel more spikes of excitement and desire. But I did.

Anchor lifted my legs, and Devotion placed a pillow under my hips. I let them move me however they wanted. Mace smacked my pussy with a tired wink.

"One more?" asked the leader, unbuttoning his pants. He looked almost stoic.

"I can go all night." I wasn't sure that was true, since I already felt so sore from being impaled on Anchor's massive cock. I hoped it was true, though.

"All right," he said. "Mouth."

Mouth crawled over me, his dark muscles rippling, softer than Anchor's. With a suggestive roll, he lowered himself so he lay on top of me. Because of the pillow, it was comfortable. Then his tongue found my pussy again.

Mace pulled Mouth's dick out from where it was trapped against my face and shoved it in my mouth. I swirled my tongue around him. Compared to the others, he was more manageable, which only made the position more enjoyable. I sucked him hard and wet while he did the same to me. I wanted to give him back some of the pleasure I experienced, but even with my effort, I doubted I felt as good to him as he did to me.

Soon, he was groaning against me, ratcheting his hips carefully up and down. I writhed but couldn't move far. He felt the best of all of them.

No, Mace did.

No, Devotion did.

Maybe Anchor?

Tickling the head of his cock with my tongue, I earned a rumble that traveled from his chest through my cunt. He hardened even more. Latching onto my clit, he sucked until I was begging and shivering. I couldn't get any words out because he filled my mouth and was in my throat and—

He tensed and shot a heavy stream into my mouth, even pausing his oral expertise to strain and bark out low notes of satisfaction. His stomach pressed against mine with frantic breaths.

"Good." The leader again. "That's all of them."

Mouth rolled off me. I felt slick everywhere. I swallowed, earning a half-smile from the leader. He'd taken off the rest of his clothes. Underneath, he looked carved from marble. Incredible.

The others stood back, recovering from their orgasms but obviously eager to return.

"Now I get you to myself." The leader cocked is head. "So beautiful. Do you need to be punished or adored or fucked until you're screaming?"

I lay there, trying to catch my breath. He actually expected me to answer?

"I've had a shitty week," I said. "Make me lose my mind, or make me feel like the goddess I am."

He chuckled darkly. "Oh, I think we can do both." He looked back at the group, who stood together so closely I wondered if they were together when no one else asked for their services. "We've been doing our best so far."

"I'll take more."

"So needy," he said, with a step forward. Stopping next to the bed, he leaned over to speak in my ear. "You haven't had my cum yet, so I'll give it to you if you're good. And, if you think you can handle it, we'll take you all at once."

My mind spun. *How?*

"Yes," I whispered, so turned on I hurt.

"Well, then." He straightened. His cock bobbed out from his body as he circled me like prey. The others watched.

The leader wasn't the longest or thickest—both of those awards went to Anchor. He wasn't strictly the most handsome—Devotion won that. Mace had the most raw sex appeal. Mouth brought me to the edge of coming the fastest.

But the leader had charisma that made it hard to look away. The other four obeyed him without question. I hung on every word, anticipated every movement.

"You're a goddess," he said, loud enough for the others to hear. "Demi-gods." He inclined his head toward the group. "I am like you. I see energy. That's my power. What's yours?"

"I can change an object's color." It was a small power, as most of them were, and it made me miss that crescent-shaped rock again.

"What do you wish you could do?"

"End this conversation so you can get on with it."

He laughed, eyes dancing. "Understood. You want to feel like a goddess. You want to hear the wet sound of your sex as I take you with all the passion and energy of a male who just... watched all of that."

My eyelids drooped. "Yes."

"Then spread your legs."

I obeyed.

He pulled the pillow forward, bringing my hips with it. "Now what do you want?"

"Fuck me."

He slapped my breast. "What do you want?"

"Fuck me."

"Say it again."

"Fuck me," I spat.

He grabbed my face and pressed his lips to mine, taking what he wanted. When his hands traveled down between my legs to trail through my slickness, I understood that he had traits of all four of the others. I arched, urging him on.

"Are you throbbing for me?" he mumbled into my mouth between kisses. "Do you want my cock to rip you open? Hm?" He thrust the head along the apex of my thighs to wet it. "Oh, you feel perfect. Warm and wet, filled with their cum, aren't you?" He licked into my mouth in a hard sweep.

Something about him dominated every part of my body. I found myself gripping the defined muscles of his back.

"Get inside me," I demanded.

And he obeyed. That was half the rush. In one push, he shoved all the way in, balls swinging against me.

I felt his heart thunder against mine.

He was done talking. All his focus consisted of rolling his body in heavy thrusts and touching every part of my skin he could reach. His palms danced across my dark nipples, trailed up into my hair, reached underneath me to squeeze my back and, further down, my ass. The way he had sex was work, adoring and stimulating my whole body while huffing out delicious groans to show his effort.

My head fell back, and his hand took advantage of the exposed neck to caress it in a dangerously firm motion.

"You're going to come with me," he said. An order he expected to be obeyed. He ground in hard and deep to punctuate his statement.

My muscles seized, on the edge of control.

"I'm going to fuck you, and you're going to come."

I didn't doubt him.

With a short nod to me, he held on tight and rammed in,

the beat rivaling the music I'd heard at the party. Fast. Athletic. And so fucking good. He got all the way in every time, claiming ownership of my pussy. That was the only way to think of it.

His panting became growls. He didn't let up. His back was sticky with sweat that I wanted to taste. He rode me like a galloping horse.

My mouth opened, involuntary. We were yelling together. The mattress bounced and all I wanted was more of this. More, more, more.

I was about to scream the word when he shouted over me, "Go!"

I did, breaking apart in a spasm of pleasure so intense I forgot where I was. He marked me, shooting in deep.

Thirsty and exhausted, I lay sprawled, too tired to move.

A broken sigh made me crane my neck to see the others. For a second, I'd forgotten about them. Devotion and Mace pumped their own cocks as they watched us. Judging from the mess on the floor, one or both had just come. It smelled like sex in here.

The leader kissed me on the jaw and awkwardly rose. It was the first awkward motion I'd seen from him. Before, he acted so in control, but I had made him wobble.

My lips curved.

After a few moments of nothing but the sound of uneven breathing, Mouth broke the silence. "All of us?"

"No," I answered before my mind caught up. I clutched the leader's hand.

He looked down at me, stoic, knowing. He didn't break eye contact. "I think we've finally tired her out."

"But that..." I swallowed. The salty residue of Mace's cum still coated my tongue.

"Was perfect," Devotion finished.

Twice the size of Devotion, Anchor jostled him with his shoulder. It looked like an inside joke between them.

The leader had already found his pants and released my hand to pull them up. I watched as the others lumbered to follow his lead or approach me.

Not bothering with clothes, Devotion and Mouth crawled on the bed and cradled my body between them, all three of us on our sides. Mouth, in my arms, traced a light path down my wrist and the back of my hand. Devotion hugged me from behind, warm and solid.

Heavy contentment flowed through my veins. Before I fell asleep, I managed to speak in a husky voice. "I want to come back."

"Free of charge," the leader said quickly. "We want you to come back too."

Through the slit in my eyelids, I saw Anchor nod.

"Come back tomorrow," Devotion whispered. "We're all yours."

Even Mace grunted in agreement.

Sore as I was, the blankets and bodies felt so comfortable that consciousness slipped away. I'd definitely return tomorrow. With these five, I felt every bit a goddess.

❧ 8 ❧

AYAME'S FIVE

Ayame returns to the five males who rocked her world.

This original story includes explicit sex, strong language, overstimulation, sex work, orgy, whips, anonymity, voyeurism, spanking, MMMMMF, DVP

Repairs and work meant I couldn't return to my group of males for several days even though I told them I'd be back tomorrow. Hopefully they weren't angry.

To be honest, it took two full days to start healing after the ride they took me on behind the party. Every night—and every day—I fantasized about Anchor's massive dick inside me or Devotion's kisses or Mace's whip. Focusing on anything else was a chore.

But chores had to be done. To wash the memory of my ex from the house, I changed the colors of the walls, inside and out, with a touch. Now, instead of a muted burnt orange, they were blue and green.

I never found the bright rock from my garden that had helped me practice my powers as a child. Remembering it still made me sad.

Compared to last week, though, the past few days saw me feeling fierce, angry, and beautiful, and ready to fuck my five again.

Today was the first day I could finally break away to the party manor without feeling on the verge of collapse. Entrance fee in hand and silky green nothing of a dress caressing my curves, I sashayed inside.

Before I even reached the door in the back, passing dancers and drinkers and musicians on the way, I went slick with anticipation.

The same horned guard from last time eyed me approaching. Confidence imbued my movements. The first time, spite had grounded me. I was better now, especially knowing there were painfully attractive men in there who wanted to pleasure me.

Said they wanted to, six days ago.

Was that still true?

"Ayame," he said. "I'm glad you've returned." Something in his tone hinted at annoyance. Had the five been asking about me?

I gave him a half-smile. "Me too."

"Males, I assume," he said, gesturing toward the correct door.

"Mm." I swept past him to push it open, blood racing.

Five heads turned to look at me. Most of them were in some state of undress as they relaxed in their common area. The bed (and chains and shower) was through another door.

Anchor, the biggest in the group in every way, stood with an intense, almost angry expression.

"You're here," Devotion cried, leaping off the shallow platform where he'd been talking with Mouth. He scooped me into his arms and planted a sensual kiss at the base of my neck. The short hair of his beard teased my skin.

The leader approached us appraisingly. Just like the last time, he was the only one completely dressed. Gold rings glinted in his ears. "You're late, goddess."

Mace's jaw tightened. He looked ready to punish me before fucking me. But damn did he look good leaning against the wall like that.

"I got here as soon as I could." I ran my hands through the back of Devotion's thick hair. He felt so good. Just having them all here was a pleasure, even if some of them weren't happy.

The leader placed his hands behind his back. Behind him, I spied Mouth handing Anchor a coin. He didn't look sad to have lost whatever bet they made.

"We don't like to be kept waiting, especially not by our favorite goddess."

His statement had me biting my lip. Still the favorite.

"Here to be fucked, are you?"

My eyes lighted on each one of them. "By all five, yes."

The leader's body language relaxed.

From the corner, Mace said in a low voice, "We have been ready to fuck you for days. Get in there."

Devotion held my hand as we went through to the far room. No sounds reached this space besides the trickle of the showering water feature on the far side of the large room and my own thundering heartbeat.

They washed my hands and feet quickly with wet cloths. As they did, the leader sat in his chair by the door, black eyes shrewd as he watched.

Even with this new frantic energy they hadn't shown when they started slow with me last time, I craved being back with them, even though they were right here.

Devotion rubbed my feet with a warm cloth, trailing fingers furtively down my ankle and foot as he did.

Mouth looked at me hungrily, sucking his bottom lip in to bite it.

Anchor stood by, his huge cock erect and ready.

Mace, with his scoundrel scar, ripped my dress off so hard it snagged and rent the fabric.

"We five," the leader narrated, "shouldn't be kept waiting. We chose this profession to give and take pleasure. And you" —his gaze raked over me with such heat I felt feverish—"let us play together. Even better." He tilted his head to the side. "Not only that, but you... your body, your eagerness..." His hand fell between his legs, but I couldn't tell if it was intentional.

At his words, enormous hands cupped my sides, lifting and placing me in a different spot on the floor. Anchor used few words. He was all power.

"Hold her," the leader instructed.

Anchor's meaty palm crushed my wrists together behind my back. Exposed in front of the group like that, with my dark nipples hard on my generous breasts, I ached for friction, for one of them to come up and fuck me already.

With a smirk that promised all kinds of sinfulness, Mace prowled up to face me.

"You see," the leader continued, "my power is to visualize energies. Since you left, there's been a change in the group."

I looked sharply away from Mace's face to focus on the leader. "What change?" I said, my voice too hoarse.

"Colors."

I frowned. I knew I could change the color of objects, but energy?

The leader waved an idle hand through the air, the one that had lain in his lap a second ago. "It's the deep red I saw on you, but now it's stuck to all of us. We all have a streak of it. Joined energy. We've been… impatient since you left."

Mace smiled, a wicked thing. His tough body swayed like a snake ready to strike. He thumbed his lip, and the look he gave was enough to make me clench my thighs to cure some of the ache. "Don't leave us again."

I hadn't noticed Mace had been holding something behind his back. The whip from before. "You're not ready to take all of us," he said, giving the whip a flick through the air. "Are you?"

"No," I answered.

"That's right." He lashed my hip enough to sting. Anchor held me firm. "You want this first, don't you?"

"Yes."

His next blow landed right on my nipple. I squeaked in pain. That only seemed to excite him. He did it again. And again, to the other. His aim was perfect.

The next crack of the whip lashed between my legs. I twisted, but that only exposed the side of my round ass to him, which he targeted next.

"Mmm," he purred. "One more thing, I think." His fingers struck out to grab my cheeks. He brought his face close to mine. He smelled spicy and delicious. The scar stretching from his eye to his thick dark hair made me weak. I always liked a bad boy. That was why I'd chosen so many and it had bitten me in the ass. And not in a fun way.

"Let her go, Anchor," said the leader.

Mace gripped my hair in a fist and led me to the humungous bed. "Lean over."

I did, making sure they all got a good view of my assets.

"Face on the blanket."

I pressed my cheek down on the soft fabric.

"You want us all to fuck you, you have to beg."

"Remember," the leader said mildly. I knew immediately what he meant. Remember that I could call this off at any point, just like the last time. I probably shouldn't trust these males, but after the ecstasy they'd given me last time and the connection we had, I'd let them do almost anything.

"I remember." Looking back at Mace, I said, "Make me beg." I had always been a goddess, but I didn't always feel like it. Today, partly because of these partners, I did.

"Bad girl," he said with feral glee. And he spanked me hard. Devotion flinched along with me. Even Mouth's eyebrow's went up.

I said nothing.

Mace hit me again, harder this time, on the other side.

I let out a broken straining noise.

"Beg," he ordered.

"I want you."

"What? Louder." His hand came down in a painful crack.

"Get inside me."

"Begging, not commands." But with his next slap, his finger dipped in, just for a second, between my cheeks. He wanted in too.

"Get your cock inside me. I want you all." My next words were halfway drowned out by the slap of Mace's spankings. "Fuck me! Fuck me! I need you all." I reached out toward the others. "Get over here."

Mouth was the first to move, crawling onto the bed in

front of me. I opened my mouth wide to let him in. He'd sucked me off so well last time, I wanted to return the favor. He glanced at Mace, whose strikes were slowing, and fisted himself. I dove for him, slurping him into my mouth. His creaky sigh of pleasure as I drew him deeper made me as wet as the bondage and spanking had done.

Mouth began to rock on the bed, thrusting between my lips.

Hands gripped my ass and the head of a new cock pushed up against my hole. The hands weren't gentle and they weren't massive. Still Mace, then. He wouldn't be polite about going slow. I braced myself. A couple movements of his feet to center himself and—*shit!*—he stabbed in deep. Right away, he shoved in hard with a relentless pace. I could hardly focus on Mouth's dick resting on my tongue when Mace took me so violently. Blankets wadded in my fist.

Then he was gone.

The change came so suddenly, I gasped, and Mouth pulled out too.

"You'll be glad I did that," Mace declared.

I looked for Devotion. He'd soothe some of the pain. As I expected, he took my hand and pulled me to my feet to kiss me.

"You said you want us all at once," the leader said.

"Yes," I answered, although it wasn't a question.

"Are you ready for that?"

My heartbeat jogged, but I wasn't about to say no.

"Yes."

"Relax for us," Devotion said coaxingly. "Open for us."

As he spoke, Mouth knelt at my feet and licked greedily between my legs. To help him, Devotion lifted one of my legs.

I sighed and leaned into Devotion as Mouth pulsed his tongue against my clit.

"We need you wetter than you've ever been."

This coming from Devotion was a surprise. He was all encouragement, adoration. That sounded like a warning.

"How can we make that happen?" He lapped at my earlobe.

It was hard to focus. Everyone but the leader was gloriously naked, and Anchor and Mace joined the two already touching me until there was a mass of hands and lips, stroking and tasting and kissing. I let waves of arousal wash over me. Someone bit my lip like fruit. Another palmed my full breast. Another roughly massaged my stinging ass.

"This," I breathed.

Bodies pressed around me. Good thing Devotion held me up because *gods!* They had muscles anyone would lust to see, much less touch. And now four were feeling every inch of my skin, exploring, rubbing against me, lightly thrusting. A chorus of sighs and moans showed how eager and sensitive they were. I found myself whimpering too.

"The bed," said the leader from where he watched.

Strong hands lifted me. I felt weightless.

"The first part is the hardest, but then you'll have all five of us at once."

Excitement rippled through the group. I squirmed in their grip. They couldn't get inside me fast enough.

Anchor lay diagonally on the bed, cock high and proud. The others laid me on top of him, face up. I would have preferred to lie the other way so I could feel his huge muscles against my belly and breasts, but I'd reached a state where they had full control.

"Arch up, beautiful," said Mace with the hint of a sneer.

I did, arching away from Anchor, who lifted my hips with

one big hand. Dizziness took me for a second, like I would fall, but he held me balanced. His stiff cock, like a fist, met my ass. On purpose. It was hard enough to settle onto his cock when he entered my pussy last time. Now he was going in the back. A moment of panic made me tense. But Anchor, for all his grim silence, was more careful than Mace. He wedged the head in, stretching me so far I must have been bleeding.

I arched harder. Mouth's tongue found my breasts and laved them carefully, enough to distract me a little from the pain of Anchor's too-large shaft.

Anchor kept fitting in little by little until the piercing pain subsided and I sat with him inside me.

"Good?" he grunted. His head was slightly above mine since he was so much taller.

I nodded, but I wasn't sure.

He rotated his hips in a few gentle thrusts. My muscles tensed every time.

Mace separated my legs so they spread wide.

Right. There was more.

"Mouth," came the leader's voice.

His tongue moved from my breasts down my stomach until his lips latched onto my sensitive nub. He detached for a second so he could give me oral on his hands and knees on the bed, stroking himself. His growls drew up more wetness, more sensitivity. No one did this like him.

Under me, Anchor moved again, small movements but obviously chasing his own pleasure. I liked that they all took as much as they gave. And I didn't feel like I was being ripped in half anymore. Stretched but not breaking.

"Keep those legs wide," said the leader, rising and coming closer.

To me, that had become a signal that the climax neared.

Mouth moaned in appreciation of my new slickness.

Devotion approached, caressing the top of my thigh. He looked wooden he was so rigid. Breaths choppy, he went next.

Finally. My pussy needed a cock to fill it. He didn't have to push hard. He slid right in. At the revelation of how wet and warm I was, he gasped and held my leg as he rolled his hips in ecstatic thrusts. Each time he slipped in all the way to the root, his groin brushed Mouth's hair, but neither seemed to mind. If anything, it aroused them more.

"Me next," said the leader, pulling his shirt over his head to expose smooth dark skin. "Careful, Devotion." He laid a hand on Devotion's firm bicep to bring him out of the sexual trance he seemed to have fallen into. Devotion pivoted so he wasn't perfectly centered. The movement made me writhe at the new position.

I blinked. Was the leader going to…?

No.

Was he?

He stripped off his pants. I'd rarely seen a hard on already leaking cum, but his was.

"Relax," said Devotion, not sounding relaxed.

The leader joined Devotion between my wide spread legs. Mouth continued to gobble me up from the side. Out of the corner of my eye, his fist worked faster.

Devotion inhaled sharply as the leader's cock met his at my center. Then, with insistent, miniature thrusts, the leader plunged inside.

I couldn't breathe. Anchor was moving and Devotion was moving and the leader was moving and all three acted more breathless and desperate than I'd ever seen. I had no more room.

"Don't forget me," said Mace. "Head back."

I couldn't take one more. Couldn't... it was too much... I was already bunching together, ready to come again and again and—

Mace grabbed my hair and pulled my head back over Anchor's shoulder. I fought for breath. But there was no time, because a dick smacked against the tongue in my open mouth.

"Open wide."

And he pumped in too.

I gagged and writhed and *gods had anything ever felt so fucking good ever?*

My whole body trembled. I wanted to see the straining faces of the others, but all I got were Mace's balls.

"Ah, that's it!" Devotion cried.

"Fuck!" from Mace.

Anchor groaned loudly and reached up for handfuls of my breasts.

The two between my legs moved unevenly, each working hard, laboring, straining for release.

Sweat covered my entire body. I was seconds away from passing out. Had to be. Five gorgeous males thrusting into me at once. If I didn't make it, who the fuck cared?

With all the cries of lifting huge weights over and over, we screamed and grunted. The men pushed in further. I had no more space to give but they found it anyway. Devotion's dick rubbed against the leader's, made slippery by my arousal. Anchor ground against my ass. Mace shoved his hard cock all the way down my throat. I breathed through my nose, eyes streaming.

With a back-arching, sight-sparkling, piercing spasm, I screamed around Mace and rode waves of orgasm so intense I thought after the third full-body shudder that it might never stop.

The first words that made sense after coming so hard were Devotion's.

"I'm coming," he gasped. He hardened, jerked, and shot a thick stream of cum inside me.

A sobbing sound of desperation broke from the leader—one of the single sexiest things I'd ever heard. His hands found my side to hold himself steady as he followed right after.

Together, they slipped out, leaving a wet mess between my legs.

Mace growled, growing more frantic until he filled my mouth. I licked his head to get it all.

Mouth moaned, bobbing with Anchor's thrusts, pumping his cock wildly. The two of them came hard at the same time. Anchor yelled, which startled me, then turned me on again.

"Fuck," I panted, hardly sounding like myself.

"Fuck," the leader echoed.

We fell in a tangle of sweaty, slippery limbs onto the bed.

Devotion faced me, pushing hair behind my ear. His pupils still filled his eyes. "You were incredible, beautiful."

"Goddess," murmured the leader.

Anchor flung his arm enough to cover most of us.

I hurt so bad and wanted that again and would take as many of them as they would let me.

"You did good," said Mace.

My chest warmed. I reached over Devotion to cup Mace's face. His normally aloof expression softened and my heart flipped over.

"Fuck, that was amazing," I breathed. Part of me knew I should get up and wash all the cum off. And blood. There was probably blood. But I couldn't move, not here between all my men.

"If I could do that every day of my life..." Mouth began.

"You'd die," said Mace.

Mouth chuckled.

"Dried out," Anchor added.

"I could go again," said Devotion, pressing closer.

The leader reached from behind me to smack Devotion lightly on the shoulder. "Give her a minute."

"Give us all a minute," said Anchor.

Devotion scooched up closer again, his chest against mine, and gave me a slow kiss on the lips.

"You can do that," I suggested.

"Turn around then." The leader didn't wait for me to obey, but flipped me over himself. Passion filled his kiss. I returned it with all the fervor I felt, exploring his full lips.

Mouth wanted a turn next. Yes, as I remembered, he was the best kisser. Technically, at least. He made my belly flutter.

Mace took my hand with a look that said he'd kill anyone who commented or made a joke.

Mouth snuggled back against Anchor's broad chest as we looked at each other.

The leader told me never to leave. How could I, when I had these five? They were addicting. They were passionate. They were everything I wanted and more.

I'd taken all five at once today.

I laughed.

"What?" Mace snapped, pulling his hand away.

"Just... you." I looked around at them all. "Swear you'll be mine."

"Already done," said the leader with a smirk.

"Swear you'll use me like you did today whenever you get the chance."

"Thenios himself couldn't stop us."

"I want to use you now." Devotion turned me back toward him. He was hard again.

I tossed my leg over his hip. My pussy ached, but I'd always want more of him. Of all of them.

Devotion slid easily into my loose center. There, in the bed with all my males watching, he fucked me again.

Apparently, I'd proven myself today. Now we could simply enjoy each other, however, whenever, and whoever we wished.

I sighed, so full of pleasure I doubted I'd ever run out.

AYAME'S REVENGE

Ayame's ex is coming back to the house, and she wants her five new partners there when it happens.

This original story includes explicit sex (including rough and revenge), strong language, fighting, MFMMMM

I surprised myself by inviting the five males I'd spent time with at the party manor over to my home. We weren't anything one could put a label on. There were five of them, for Divine's sake. Plus, we didn't even know each other's real names.

There was the leader, a dark-skinned virtuoso, watching and guiding every session.

Mace, with his dark hair and roguish scar, made me wet before he even began punishing me.

Anchor filled my dreams and my pussy with the biggest dick I'd ever sat on.

Mouth lived up to his name and could get me off so fast with his expert tongue.

And there was Devotion, the romantic who openly adored my body, showering it with kisses and tender lovemaking.

Together, they were mind blowing. I craved them. Even when I was supposed to focus on other tasks, my mind wandered back to the scents and sounds and *feel* of them.

We were never going to be more than luxurious fucking partners. And yet...

When I heard rumors that my ex was returning to the house, I wanted them with me. I couldn't tell if it was for comfort or validation or just a giant fuck you to the one who had mocked me for my losses a couple months ago. Honestly, I didn't care. Maybe I wanted my men around for all three reasons.

Four.

Four reasons.

We would obviously fuck here too, and the idea made me giddier than it should have. Also making me giddy today was the prospect of my ex's face when five powerful males stared at him like they wanted to kill him.

My heartbeat chased itself unevenly as I tidied up. Gods knew my ex didn't deserve to see the house looking nice—he didn't even deserve to be remembered by name—but I liked everything clean. I was doing just fine without his sorry ass. Organizing and cleaning also gave me something to do with the time between now and when my men would show up.

When I told them where I lived, Mace clarified directions for the others, as if he already knew exactly where to find me. I shouldn't have liked that. But I liked a lot of things I shouldn't lately.

Like getting railed by five gorgeous males at once. There was nothing like it. I loved taking them one by one, by twos, threes, four, or all five. Some configurations took longer to recover from—I was down to one day off if they wanted double or triple penetration.

My eyes fell on the front room. It was a little smaller than the space where the five and I regularly had steamy trysts. There were bigger rooms in the back of my house. This wasn't a manor like many other gods had, but it was large for only one person. At the center of the house was an open, tiled area filled with plants. I should have put my colorful rock garden there instead of defenseless in the back where rains could wash it away.

The reason I stayed within sight of the front room was the generous window that allowed me to see people coming to the main door.

What if my ex showed up first?

My stomach flipped at the idea. After he'd laughed at me for losing one of my most precious possessions, one that reminded me not only of my power but of life as a little girl in Menos, many things became clear. I'd made excuses for him, assumed he was having a bad day, didn't understand the importance of what I needed, required more communication, wasn't the same after a few drinks, and on and on and on. In hindsight, his heartlessness might have been a blessing. It gave me the strength I needed to kick him out.

He wasn't confused or misunderstood or having a bad day. He was an asshole.

"Your energy is all over this place," a smooth voice declared.

I whipped around. The leader, dressed in a brown suit, slipped his hands in his pockets as he surveyed the colorful space. He looked good enough to eat.

"Thank you for inviting us," he said, approaching and

giving me a kiss. He smelled fresh, like soap. I nuzzled into his neck and he held me.

None of the others came with him.

"Where's everyone else?" I asked.

The leader chuckled. "Always so greedy. We need to do something about that." He released me to continue peering around. The way he looked was like someone inspecting property they might buy someday or visit on a vacation. "Dark red everywhere," he said.

The walls in this room were blue. I did have some accents that were dark red, but he was talking about my aura, the mark I left on things. According to him, my energy had rubbed off on all five of the men after I visited the first time.

He spun to face me again. "So this... boyfriend of yours—"

"Ex."

"Of course. Ex. When is he coming?"

I loved the dangerous, powerful way he spoke those words. I heard the reined-in possessiveness, the anger at the hints I'd dropped about my ex's bad behavior.

"I'm not sure. I only know it's today, sometime." I chewed the inside of my lip. When I realized I was doing it, I stopped with a mental curse. Where was the confidence I'd recovered the past few weeks? Why did my ex still have the power to tear it all down?

The leader hummed deep in his throat. "I see. What is he?"

"Demi-god."

The leader's lips curled up. The gleeful threat in them warmed my belly. Another thing I shouldn't want—revenge taken by my new... what? Partners?

"Very good," he said.

"I'm not asking you to do anything except be here with me today."

"Oh," he said, stalking closer, "we'll be with you however and whenever you want." He drew close to my ear, giving me a new chance to smell his warm, clean scent. "Fuck him. In fact..." He took my hand and pulled me toward the big front window. "Your eyes keep going here. Is this where he'll arrive?"

"I think so." It felt strange to have the leader in my front room. He and the others belonged in that back room at the party. Now I was mixing them with my real life. Did I want the leader asking questions about my ex? Did I want them to be more than anonymous partners in the best group sex I'd ever had? Relationships were complicated. They were dangerous. My muscles tightened at the thought of them.

But also, I didn't want to let the five go. I felt at least as possessive of them as they did of me.

Speaking of that, why had the others not come yet? Had someone else paid for their services? I felt stupid for never having considered it before. But now that I thought about it, I hated the idea of any of them fucking someone other than me. Unless it was each other. For some reason, that felt allowed.

I was so fucking selfish.

"Where'd you go? You're not with me." The leader traced my cheekbone with a finger.

"I'm thinking."

"Think with me." He slung an arm around my waist to look out the window with him. "Imagine him appearing right there." He pointed.

Frowning, I turned from the tree-strewn path visible through the window to shoot a look at the leader.

He appeared perfectly calm. Amused, even. "Imagine this is what he sees." He cupped my cheek and kissed my neck.

Eyes closed, I sank into the sensation of his lips trailing down my throat.

"You don't belong to him. You belong to us," he murmured. "Now bend down. Face the window and bend over."

I did as he said.

The leader moved behind me and pulled down the short pants I wore. "Keep looking. What would he think if he knew you were getting fucked right now?" The head of his cock teased my entrance, which was getting wetter and needier by the second. "Would he be jealous?"

I gripped the windowsill tight. Desire shot through me, making me throb. "Please," I begged.

"Please what?"

"Do it."

He gripped my hair firmly but not enough to hurt. "Keep looking. Please what?"

"Fuck me."

"You want me to ram into you where your ex can see? You're a bad girl."

"Do it, please." He was making me crazy.

Finally, he gave me what I needed. With a few sharp thrusts that sent me bobbing toward the window, he fit all the way inside. His grip on my hair hadn't lessened.

I gasped as he smacked into me, balls swinging. His heavy breathing became possessive growls of need. My favorite thing was the leader when he turned feral.

"Whose are you?" he demanded.

"Mine."

I heard dark laughter in his next few panting breaths. "And then?"

"Yours."

"That's right. You deserve better than that fucker. Now he can't do this." He punctuated the statement with a hard, deep plunge. "Or share this perfect body." He reached around to grab my hanging tits through my clothes.

My sensitive nipples chafed against the cloth as he kneaded me. I whimpered, needing more of him.

"He didn't understand... what a goddess you are. Keep looking!" he snapped.

My eyelids kept drifting closed so I could focus on the delicious feeling of his hard cock sliding ruthlessly inside me. "Yes."

"Imagine we could see him now. How he'd hate this." He ground against me in a ferocious rhythm.

I cried out, all words leaving.

"I bet he'd hate this more," Devotion interjected, standing between me and the window and making me straighten. My yip of surprise at his arrival was swallowed by his worshipful mouth.

The leader kept pounding me from behind, which meant I had to stay slightly bent to let him in, but Devotion compensated by leaning forward. He kissed like a lover returning from years away. It didn't matter than I kept rocking against him to the beat of the leader's thrusts. If anything, that seemed to add to Devotion's fervor. It had only been a couple days, but I'd missed his tongue and his adoration.

Devotion's fingers inched down, finding my swollen folds and rubbing the exact spot I wanted. I seized and gulped in a breath. Devotion caught it in a kiss deeper than before.

The leader felt me getting close too, judging from his punishing strokes. Gods, I loved this.

"So wet," Devotion moaned.

Behind me, the *smack smack smack* grew frenzied.

"So needy."

I groaned loudly.

"That's it," said the leader. "Come for me."

Squeezing his cock hard, I burst apart in their arms. My shout was loud enough for anyone near the house to hear.

The leader finished, shoving deep as if to mark me as his. When he slipped out with a sigh, I turned to kiss him. He pulled his pants up and met my lips.

"That's my girl," he muttered.

Devotion, dropping to his knees, pulled my short pants up for me.

"That's okay," I told him, pulling them up the rest of the way. He only gave me a dimpled smirk, kissed my exposed thigh, and rose.

Devotion wore an open vest and long, fawn-colored pants. Nearly every time I went to meet them, he preferred to be naked. I preferred that too. But I supposed we couldn't have sex all the time in the real world.

Tell that to yourself five minutes ago.

My face and neck felt hot from all the attention.

The leader looked out the window again. "Too bad he didn't get here to see that."

I chuckled, much less stressed than I had been before they arrived. I wanted all five of them to come stay with me and never leave. "I would have given my left foot for him to show up just then."

Devotion leaned in close enough for his breath to mingle with mine. "We'll give him something to see, don't worry."

A pleasant shiver ran down my backbone.

"Come here, you—" The last word, something foul, got cut off by the sound of things falling.

My kitchen!

I tore through the house. I'd made sure no servants remained in the house—I had a couple who came in for cleaning and cooking once a week—so they'd be out of the way when my ex arrived. So the voice wasn't a servant. It wasn't my ex.

But it did sound familiar. Its natural language was command.

"Mace," I huffed, rounding the corner into the little space. I wasn't much of a cook myself, so I hadn't expanded the kitchen over the decades. More surprising than the fallen plates were the three figures sprawled in different positions.

Mace stood wearing all black (I could have guessed), feet far apart, hair sensually mussed, glaring down at Mouth and Anchor who looked like they'd been startled out of doing something unsanitary only seconds ago. Mouth's lips were wet and his parted mouth revealed an eager tongue. Anchor looked flushed. Also, his dick was out.

So I was right. Mouth and Anchor. Which of the others were together? The thought of the males hooking up didn't bother me like the thought of them taking on a sixth when I wasn't there. I was just glad they had all arrived.

Mace's reckless gaze found me. "There you are."

When he prowled toward me, I felt like prey in the best way.

"I couldn't wait anymore." His fingers circled my neck hard enough that I couldn't move but could still breathe. He gave me a brutal, demanding kiss. The ache returned between my legs. "They were taking too long." He flung his head in the direction of Mouth and Anchor, who had gotten to their feet and were still adjusting their clothes.

After the initial surprise of being dumped in an unfamiliar place, they showed no embarrassment. Their confusion and arousal were starting to give way to delight at seeing me.

"Sorry he interrupted," I said.

The leader stroked my back affectionately.

Mace spoke over whatever Mouth was going to say. "He's not here yet, is he?"

My smile dimmed. "No."

The tension in Mace's shoulders released a fraction. "I told them we were leaving. They were taking too long. I kept picturing that fucker here and I..." His hands clenched into fists.

"We obviously wanted to be here before him too," said Mouth. "Anchor's good in a fight." He gave him a fond look.

Anchor scowled. "We took too long. We're here now."

"That's all right," I said. "Help yourself to any food." My pantry overflowed with more things than I could eat alone. Long-lasting food had sat there since before my ex left. Since it felt wasteful to throw it out, the damned jars and stacks of hard bread had sat there. I wasn't about to touch it.

"Later," said the leader, but the others were already grabbing snacks.

Strange that it felt natural to have them raiding my kitchen.

"What is this ruckus? Ayame, do you have people over?"

My chest constricted.

My ex was here.

"Fuck," I breathed. Instead of the anger I expected to feel, nerves raced through my limbs.

The leader's expression didn't change. He tilted up his chin. "That him?"

For some reason, I could exhale. "Yeah."

"Ability? Forgot to ask."

The others poked their heads out of the pantry as they caught onto what was happening. Mace stuffed his food away to come to my side.

"He doesn't have one."

The leader's smile was venomous. "Even better."

"Ayame, what—?" My ex froze at the sight of five well-built deathless males in the kitchen with me. He wore a cream-yellow shirt I'd bought him two years ago because I thought it complemented his dark skin. It had a new stain.

He rounded on me. "Who are all these people?"

My mind rapidly sized him up compared to the others. He was taller than Mouth, shorter than Anchor or Mace... Problem was, I knew my ex and all the things he was likely to do, but I didn't know the five very well outside the bedroom.

"Friends," I said. Close enough.

Mace fairly bristled with rage. Devotion took my hand.

My ex watched as I slipped my fingers through Devotion's. Even though he got angrier, the warm weight of the hand holding mine steadied me.

"Friends?" he mocked. "Ayame, how dare you invite men to our house—"

"My house," I corrected. "So get whatever you came for and get out."

"I wasn't coming for my things," he said stepping closer.

Mouth, Anchor, and the leader arranged themselves protectively in front of me.

"The fuck is this?" he spat. "Did you get yourself a little army?"

I liked that description, but I refused to answer. I owed him nothing. If my ex were smart, he'd back away. But he wasn't. So he kept staring at us all with the air of someone ready to throw a punch.

"I knew you were a fucking whore. Are you all sleeping with her?"

Devotion landed the first hit. I expected Mace to fight

first. It delighted me that Devotion cared enough about me to give my ex what he deserved after those comments.

My ex pinwheeled his arms, jerking and kicking, but six against one weren't good odds, even for a fit demi-god like him. He threw a punch that landed on Mouth's face. Catching my ex's hand as he retracted it, Anchor palmed his fist so hard a series of pops cracked through the air. I winced as my ex let out a scream. Mace smiled savagely and moved Anchor to have a better shot at him.

It was chaos. Finally, I heard real fear in my ex's voice. In desperation, he lashed out at me, grazing my knee with a savage kick. I fell to the ground.

The backlash from my five was so intense my ex was semi-conscious in seconds. Watching his eyes partially close and his head bob only made me angrier. This useless, controlling vermin of a male held so much sway over me even now.

My leg shot with pain as I forced myself upright. Mouth noticed me enough to move out of the way, apparently guessing what I was going to do.

The leader punched my ex in the face and then noticed me too. He took a step back.

My ex focused blearily on me, disgust contorting his swelling features.

"Fuck you!" I cried and hurled my fist against his eye.

My leg seized and I fell back down, hand stinging too. He fell a moment afterward.

"They're better than you ever were," I spat.

He didn't move or respond.

"Wait. Is he…?" I craned to see if his chest was moving.

Mace wiped his nose with the back of his hand. "Unless you want him not to be, then I can deal with that for you."

"No, not... for now." I didn't want him dead. Bleeding on my floor surrounded by five protectors felt good enough.

The ground tilted and I shot into the air. A shriek built in my belly before I realized it was Anchor. He cradled me in his beefy arms.

"I know a sprite who'll fuck him up when he wakes," the leader said, uncharacteristically frazzled. He straightened the gold in his ears and his brown suit.

"Are you all right?" Devotion asked behind us. When I tilted my head back, I saw him speaking to Mouth, who was holding his jaw in obvious discomfort.

Mouth shook his head like a dog shaking off water. "I'll be fine. Worth it."

Devotion hugged Mouth sideways and caught up with me. "And you, my love?"

"It's barely anything. He just knocked me down."

His muscles relaxed.

"Where do you want me to put you down?" Anchor asked. His huge blunt face peered down into mine. Unlike the others, he was bald, and he wore the look well.

I was about to say *my bedroom* but my bed wasn't large enough for us all, so I paused. "Here's fine. I can probably stand."

We stood in the open courtyard with foliage. Sun shone down through a square opening in the ceiling.

Anchor didn't oblige. "Something for Mouth and Mace?"

Mace had acted so exhilarated by the fight that I hadn't noticed the blood on his arms and neck.

"Are you all right?" I asked him.

He gave an evil toothy smile. "Never better. Glad we were there to put in a word or two of our own."

"You did beautifully," Devotion said, taking my hand.

"And no one—*no one*—says that shit to one of ours," the leader put in.

One of ours. I liked the sound of that. Murmurs of agreement from the others told me they did too.

"Need something cold, Mouth?" Anchor asked.

"No, I work just fine. Sore is all," came the answer. He stretched his jaw. It looked a little red, but not broken. It would heal.

"I'm taking you to your room," said Anchor.

The others perked up like dogs scenting food.

"You don't even know where it is," I laughed.

"You forget," said the leader, "that I see energy. It's right over there."

Damn it, he pointed in the right direction. Anchor followed his lead. I didn't want to argue anymore. I wanted soft blankets and my five around me and my ex gone. The adrenaline from the fight was wearing off, and my soul and body felt heavy.

Mace trotted forward, not tired at all, but vibrant as an animal over its kill. "I'll take care of the mess for you. Don't want me to finish him?"

"Mm..."

"Bound and left somewhere remote? Or bound to watch our fun? I'm happy to do either."

Mace really did sound happy. It was concerning. And yes, hot.

For a second, I wanted to have my ex see what real communication and satisfaction meant during sex, but I doubted I could get off if he stared furiously at me. Sometimes the fantasies were just that, and reality had to be different.

"Somewhere remote."

With a nod, he leapt back the way we'd come.

"Do you think he'll take him to the Far Realm?" I asked Devotion, who still held my hand.

"More important," said the leader, "Ayame."

Mouth, despite his injury, tasted the name too, relishing the syllables under his breath.

"Yes," I said, uncomfortably, although I didn't need to be uncomfortable. I liked our anonymous arrangement. Predictably, my ex had ruined it. For once, it wasn't his fault. Of course he was going to use my name. In the storm of thoughts and emotions leading up to his arrival, that fact simply slipped my mind.

"It's a beautiful name," the leader said.

"I've heard of you."

I looked up at Anchor in surprise. I had some fame, but the idea of these five hearing about me outside of our unique situation took me aback.

He shrugged a shoulder the size of my head. "Your rock garden. I create and maintain roads. Your rock garden was something we'd talk about, because no one had anything like it. It looked good."

I found myself getting choked up.

Also, Anchor maintained roads? I should have considered that the men might have had extra jobs in addition to being elite erotic partners.

"Thank you. I liked it too."

We reached my bedroom down a hallway that was now green. Inside was a riot of multi-colored pillows, a multi-colored bedspread beneath a multi-colored canopy, one wall with a large inset terrarium, and solid black accents.

"Ayame," Devotion said in awe, releasing my hand so Anchor could set me down.

I assessed the size of the bed. Maybe three, four at most,

could fit on the mattress comfortably. Not six. But the familiar blanket felt incredibly soothing.

I stretched, arching my back and reaching my arms over my head.

"I'm surprised you don't wear more colors like this," said Mouth, fingering the curtain of the canopy while eyeing my curves with open appreciation.

"I like to stand out next to them."

"Mm." Devotion kissed me. "You could do that wearing a rag."

"Or nothing," Mouth added.

I arched up to return Devotion's passionate kiss. He was so beautiful and explored my mouth with such need. I opened my legs so he could stand between them as he leaned over me. Cupping my face, he opened his mouth wide, needing more of me. I needed more of him—more of him on my lips, his hands on my body, his bulge grinding against my aching core.

"Give her to me," Mace demanded.

Back already.

I opened my eyes in time to see him throw Devotion off me. Mace looked wild and wicked and feral in a way that frightened me. His chest heaved. One arm had torn off his black outfit, revealing flexed muscles. The scar on his eyebrow slashed dangerously into his hair.

He aroused me so much my belly clenched with desperation.

"She's not even naked yet," he snapped. His attention locked onto me. "You know what I just did for you?" His fingers ripped at my clothes, yanking them off.

I didn't help. I enjoyed seeing him like this, getting frustrated. Needing me more and more. "No. What?"

"I dragged your boyfriend to the Nalian swamps." He ripped off my last piece of clothing.

That was far—the next Realm over the sea—but close enough to return if he wanted to. The disappointment that settled over me suggested I did want Mace to kill my ex after all.

"He wanted to fight." Mace's eyes never left mine as he pulled his cock free from his pants. "You all weren't there." My skin prickled at his words and his stiff dick demanding access.

I cried out as he pushed his thick cock ruthlessly deep. The rest of his story evaporated as he thrust hard, growling, taking.

I tried to hold onto something, but his sex was so rocky I couldn't do anything but let go. A scream clawed at my throat.

Mace pulled me closer with deathless strength, wedging himself further inside. The others let him claim me with brutal strokes. He was already so hard when he began fucking me that it didn't take him long to come. Almost angrily, he shoved in, pushing his spurts of cum deep.

Sweat covered my quickly rising chest as he pulled out, wiping his face with a fist.

"Is he alive?" the leader asked Mace calmly.

"He wanted to fight me. I was happy to fight him." Mace smiled for the first time, an evil smirk with a peek of teeth. His gaze flashed to mine and back to the leader.

"Shouldn't have left him alone," Anchor muttered.

"No," I said, trying to catch my breath. "We should have." I caught Mace's eye and didn't smile exactly, but I crinkled my eyes in ferocious encouragement.

Mace's grin widened. He tucked himself back in his pants.

"Wicked girl," said the leader approvingly. "You want five males to fuck you *and* you want revenge?"

"Do you feel well enough for that?" Devotion butted in.

My pussy throbbed from Mace's intrusion. I lay flopped open on the bed, legs hanging over the side. And the leader's question turned me on so hard I felt like begging. "Yes, I do. I want it all."

"We have all night," said Mouth eagerly.

"You deserve to be pleasured after today," Devotion added, trailing fingertips over the top of my thigh.

"She does," the leader agreed. He approached in his signature smooth manner and keen eye. He wanted a wild night too.

"What are you waiting for?" Mace barked. "She says she wants to be fucked. Fuck her."

Lying spread wide for my five males, I couldn't have agreed with him more.

Thank you for reading *Lovers and Monsters*! Please consider leaving a review. Reviews help authors like me get found by more readers.

Sign up for my newsletter to read *Wings and Blindness*—an Eros and Psyche remix that asks what would happen if Psyche were sent to kill Eros from the beginning...

This first book in the Deathless Love series welcomes you to the Eight Realms, where danger and desire lurk in every corner, and mythology isn't quite as you remember it.

Join the Foxy newsletter and read this book FREE!

READ MORE BY ZORA FOX

Fae and Shadow duology
  End of the Forest
  Trapped by the Fae

Deathless Love—novels
  Wings and Blindness
  Flowers and the Far Realm
  Flame and Warpaint
  Temptation and Tridents

Deathless Love—novellas
  Storm and Sanctuary
  Full Moons and Vampires
  Candle Wax and Sunlight

9 781950 041428